The Adventures of ELT The Super Dog

The Adventures of ELT The Super Dog

DANIEL R. PARD

AuthorHouse™ LLC
1663 Liberty Drive
Bloomington, IN 47403
www.authorhouse.com
Phone: 1-800-839-8640

Published by AuthorHouse 01/02/2014

ISBN: 978-1-4918-1232-7 (sc)
ISBN: 978-1-4918-1231-0 (hc)
ISBN: 978-1-4918-1230-3 (e)

Library of Congress Control Number: 2013915895

ACKNOWLEDGMENTS

I wish to thank Kimberly Charette-Pard for the front cover art and Brad Pard for the map art.

Downtown Spring Valley

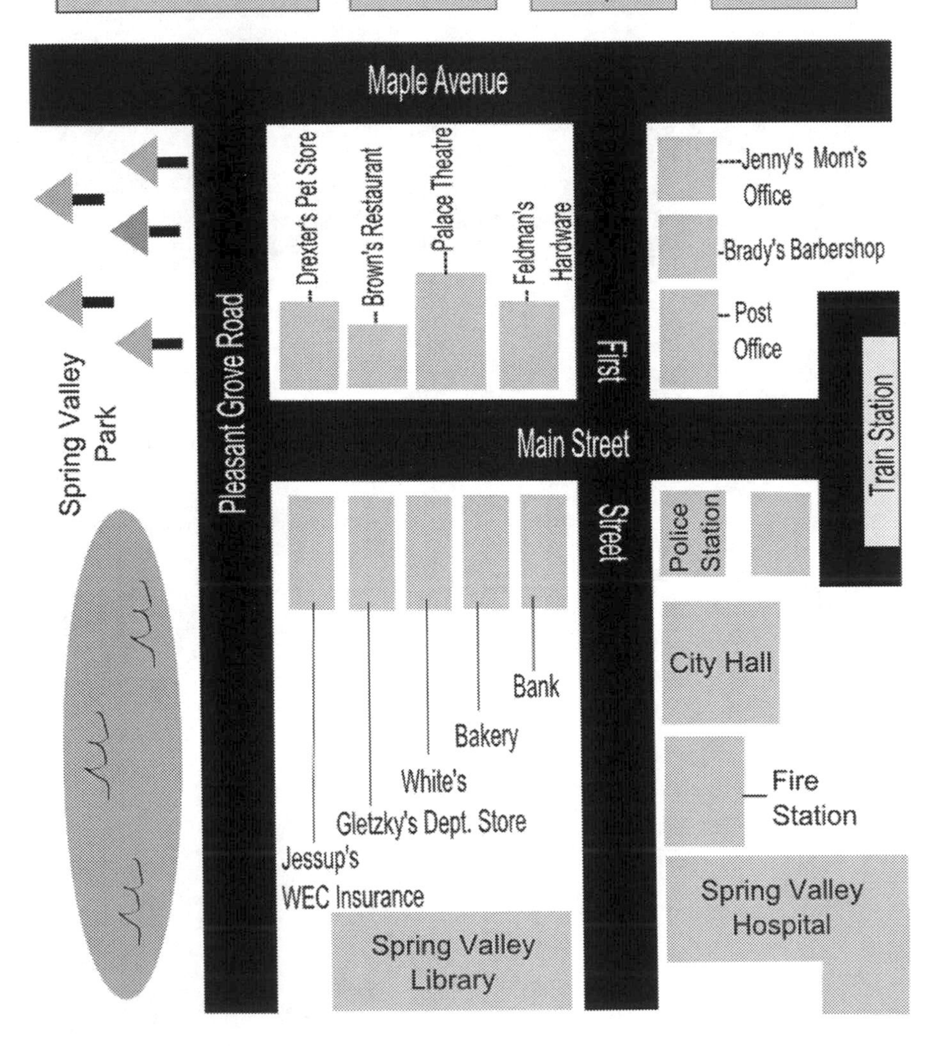

Ralph's Neighborhood

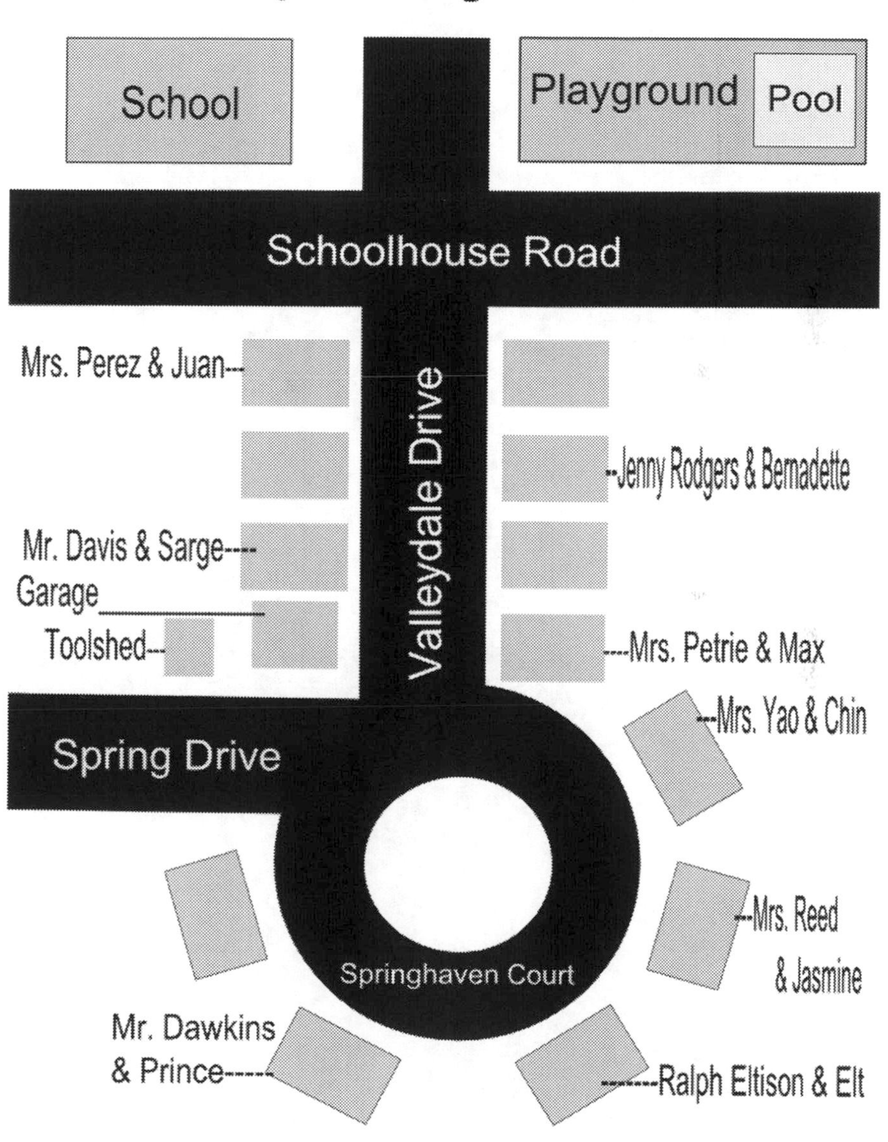

CHAPTER 1

"SURRENDER AT ONCE DR. PLASMO!" yelled Mr. Magnificent.

"Never!" declared the super villain. "There's nothing you can do to save all of these poor innocent kids, caped blunder!"

The yellow, fair-haired young superhero scouted the scene before him. The kids of the fourth grade class at Spring Valley Elementary School were in deep trouble. Mrs. Randolph, one of the school's fourth grade teachers, didn't know what to do. Her class was outside the school and couldn't get back in, they were trapped by the presence of the evil doctor's plasmo ray gun. He was about to fire his ray upon them when the town's favorite caped wonder was about to save the day.

Mr. Magnificent flew down in front of the class as the villain fired his ray gun. If struck by the dangerous rays, all of the students would be turned into jelly. Mr. Magnificent blocked the ray with his super shield-like cape. The ray deflected off the cape and back at Dr. Plasmo, almost transforming him into jelly.

Dr. Plasmo's evil helicopter swirled by. The mad doctor jumped in. Before he jetted off, Dr. Plasmo shook his fist at the superhero.

"You may have foiled my dreadful plan today, Mr. Magnificent," blasted Plasmo. "But I will be back to take over your school!"

The helicopter flew away. The kids rejoiced as Mr. Magnificent soared around the school, and then exited in a flash.

"Oh, Mr. Magnificent!" declared Mrs. Randolph. "You saved the day again, but Ralph, you need to write the question down on the board . . . ."

The kids around Mrs. Randolph laughed out loud and stared at Mr. Magnificent. The superhero was confused. He took off his black mask, revealing his true identity as one Ralph Eltison, age ten, and a student himself at Spring Valley Elementary School.

"Ralph, I'm going to ask you one more time," stated the teacher. "Could you please write the question on the board?"

Ralph Eltison snapped out of his daydream. He was standing up in front of his desk staring about, not realizing that he had been standing there for over three minutes. The kids in his classroom figured he was daydreaming, for it had happened before.

Mrs. Randolph had asked Ralph to write one of the science test review questions on the board, and answer the question of course. But sometime between a few minutes before she asked him and the moment he was in front of the class, Ralph started daydreaming about Mr. Magnificent, his alter-ego, or at least his imaginary superhero friend.

Ralph didn't know what the question was. He had no idea where they were in the book, so he continued to stand there, frozen.

"Hey Ralph, let us know what planet you came from," said fellow classmate Sam Meyers. "What a loser."

The kids laughed at Sam's remark. Not because it was so funny, they laughed because it was cool to laugh at the Eltison kid. More importantly, they were afraid of Sam the bully.

"Okay Mr. Meyers," said Mrs. Randolph. "We don't need any of your input on this matter."

Mrs. Randolph turned her attention back to Ralph.

"Ralph, why don't you pack your things and go visit Mr. Hurley," she continued.

Kids around Ralph began to "ooh" and "ahh", the way kids do when one of their friends or classmates was in trouble. Ralph bowed his head and slowly gathered his books and pencils. He stuffed them into his book bag and walked over to Mrs. Randolph. She handed him a yellow slip of paper, the same yellow paper that an unruly kid gets when he or she has to visit the principal.

When Ralph passed by one of his fellow students, Jenny Rodgers, she too bowed her head. She was the best friend Ralph had, and she barely talked to him. But she was one of the only kids that wasn't mean to Ralph. She felt bad for him, she knew he was going to get in some kind of trouble. Daydreaming shouldn't warrant too serious of a punishment, but this wasn't the first time it had happened. The school year had just started, and already Ralph Eltison was visiting the principal, Mr. Hurley, for the third time.

Surely Ralph's dad was going to find out about it. Ralph hoped that his dad wouldn't have to pick him up from school. Not that Ralph's dad had to travel a long way to get to the school and miss out on a day's work. No, Mr. Eltison worked from home, and home was only a couple of blocks from school.

It was just that Ralph didn't want his dad to know. Ralph didn't want to disappoint him. Ralph wanted his dad to be proud of him. The school year had just started. How could he have done this daydreaming thing three times in less than two weeks?

Luckily, all that happened was a phone call from Mr. Hurley to Mr. Eltison. His dad had found out, but at least he didn't have to pick Ralph up from the principal's office.

There was no punishment, and for a good reason. Ralph had been through quite a bit, and he was having trouble coping with some things.

As the school bell rang and classes had ended, Ralph made his way home. He probably wouldn't see Sam Meyers on the way home. There were very few times that Ralph had to deal with Sam Meyers, but when he did, Sam was big trouble. He wanted no part of Sam today, especially with all he had been through earlier.

Ralph usually walked to and from school alone every day. Sometimes he was accompanied by his classmate, Jenny Rodgers. She was really the only friend Ralph had. In the morning, he trekked his way to school without any interruptions.

Ralph lived pretty close to school. He lived on Springhaven Court, a circled road that led to into Valleydale Drive. Valleydale then crossed with Schoolhouse Road, where the school was situated at the corner. It was about a ten to fifteen minute walk, and he always walked to school, unless the weather was inclement.

On the way home, Ralph traveled back the way he came, but he made several stops along the way; he didn't have to rush home in the afternoon the way he rushed to school in the morning. What did he do on the way home that took a little extra time? He visited the neighborhood pets.

The first pet was Juan the Chihuahua. His owner was Mrs. Perez, who lived on the corner of Schoolhouse Road and Valleydale Drive. Juan was always very excited when Ralph stopped by. He always waited for Ralph on his front porch. Ralph would stoop down and pet Juan through the fence holes. Ralph's hands were always coated with many kisses and licks. He would spend about five minutes with Juan before moving on to his next friend.

Two houses down, on the corner of Spring Drive and Valleydale Drive, (which was also connected to Ralph's road, Springhaven Court) lived Sarge the Boxer. Sarge was the pride and joy of Mr. and Mrs. Davis, a retired couple. Sarge was not the same excitable, lovable bundle of energy like Juan, but he was very happy to receive a daily visitor. Instead of running and jumping his way to greet Ralph, the Boxer would slowly walk over to him. Ralph would shake hands through the fence holes, talk to the Boxer, and finish with a piece of food that Ralph would wrap up from lunch. Sarge loved food, both human and canine.

Ralph would then go visit Max the Sheepdog, who lived across the street from Sarge. Max's owner was Mrs. Petrie, who was retired and lived alone. Now Max was up in age, so he was not always outside waiting for Ralph. The hotter it was, the more likely that Max was inside enjoying the air conditioning. But on the days that Max was under the front awning, he would slowly make his way down to meet his human friend. Ralph would only stay a few minutes, for he knew Max was getting up in years, and he didn't want to tire the old boy out. Ralph did love to reach over the fence and pull the hair from over Max's eyes so he could see the Sheepdog's brown beauties.

Next to Mrs. Petrie lived Mrs. Yao. She owned an orange Chow Chow named Chin. He was rarely in the front yard. He stayed in his doghouse mostly. Ralph never stopped by to pet him, but sometimes the boy and the Chow Chow would eye each other. Ralph would stand in front of Chin's yard, and the Chow Chow would stare back at him from the backyard.

The last stop was Ralph's next door neighbor, Mrs. Reed, who was the only cat owner in the neighborhood dominated by dog owners. Her cat's name was Jasmine. Jasmine was a short-haired tabby; brown, gray, and a touch of orange in her fur.

Jasmine would always come up to her fence and jump, balancing herself along the top of the fence while Ralph passed by. He would stop by and pet Jasmine. She would return the favor. Jasmine would leap down on his side of the fence, lie down on her back, and let Ralph rub her belly.

Jasmine would sniff Ralph's hand. She could tell all the places that Ralph had been that day before he met her, for she knew all the neighborhood dogs very well. Being a cat, and mainly an outside one, she would leave her yard and visit the other dogs. They basically tolerated her. At first, Sarge would chase her, but he grew tired of never catching the feline.

On the other side of Ralph's house lived Mr. Dawkins. He owned a Doberman Pinscher named Prince. Mr. Dawkins took Prince to dog shows, and he won quite a few competitions. Ralph was always intimidated by Prince's stern appearance, and never tried to pet him.

Prince was a "chip off his owner's block." Mr. Dawkins loved his dog, and thought that his dog was better than anyone else's. So that feeling kind of rubbed off on Prince. He thought he was better than Sarge and the other dogs in the neighborhood. Ralph would see Mr. Dawkins walk his dog around the block sometimes, and he would wave. There was only one time that Ralph could remember that Mr. Dawkins would offer to let Ralph pet his prized possession.

Ralph enjoyed visiting these pets. Although the contact with these loving animals made him happy for the moment, Ralph would sadden once he walked into his own yard.

Ralph longed for a pet of his own. He loved cats, but he really loved dogs. He had told his dad about wanting a dog, and there was quite a discussion in the Eltison household about getting one, but all the talk about a dog ceased when the sad and terrible event happened in Ralph's and his dad's lives.

Ralph was eight at the time, and he was in the second grade. His dad worked in an office building downtown, and his mom stayed home to raise Ralph. There was talk about adding a sister or brother to the family, and even a pet. But one day Ralph came home and found his dad home early from work. He was on the phone talking with someone. It seemed very important, and his mom was nowhere to be seen.

After Ralph's dad finished his phone call, he sat down and talked with his son. He told Ralph the news and it wasn't good. Ralph's mom was in the hospital, and was very sick. Ralph had noticed that his mom had not been feeling well for about a week, but he figured she had the flu. Ralph's dad explained to Ralph that he had taken Mrs. Eltison to the doctor's office that day. The doctor informed Mrs. Eltison that she needed to go to the hospital to receive medical treatment.

What followed was a very trying and sad time for the family. Mrs. Eltison came home from the hospital. Ralph thought she was better, but she was still sick, and she would soon have to go back.

By the time Ralph almost turned nine, Mrs. Eltison stayed at the hospital. Ralph would visit her and thought she was coming home, but she never did. On the day that she left forever, Ralph was at school. Ralph's grandparents were at the house, waiting for him to come home from school. Ralph's dad had to stay at the hospital and make arrangements for Mrs. Eltison's final resting place.

Ralph was too young to understand why he lost his mom and why he wasn't going to get a sister or brother. All the talk about getting a dog took a back seat because of Mrs. Eltison's illness. Mr. Eltison tried to spend as much time as he could with his son, but he needed to change some things so he could raise his son on his own.

Ralph's dad started his own business, and started working from home. There he could do his work while Ralph was at school, and be home for his boy when school was over. Ralph's grandparents lived across town, so if Mr. Eltison had to be away, he had Ralph's child care covered.

A year had passed since Ralph's mom died. It was now September in Spring Valley and school had just started. Ralph would be turning ten years old in the middle of October. Since Ralph did not have many friends, he often turned to his imagination. He made up Mr. Magnificent in his head, pretending he was the superhero that fought villains like Dr. Plasmo. Having an imaginary friend like Mr.

Magnificent was okay for a nine year-old, but not good if imaginary friends were taking place of school work.

Ralph's dad had asked Ralph what he wanted for his birthday. Ralph was skittish at first, for he knew that wanting a dog for his birthday would probably put stress on his dad. One night at dinner, Ralph just "put it out there" for his dad to chew on.

"Dad, I know what I really want for my birthday."

Ralph's dad had no clue.

"Great, any ideas would be helpful," replied Mr. Eltison.

"Well dad, I want a dog," said Ralph. "A kind of big one, not too big you know, just big enough for me to take care of."

Ralph's dad was quiet for a few seconds. He bit into a piece of steak and chewed. He then swallowed the piece.

"A dog is a very big responsibility," said his dad.

Ralph knew it was coming. The old "big responsibility" line.

"You know you have to feed it, give it water, groom, bathe, clean up after, and pick up after it does its business," Ralph's dad continued. "Then there's walking it, and potty training it. Are you sure you can handle that?"

Ralph's dad knew then that he really wanted a dog, but he also knew that his boy would only be ten. Maybe he fed him enough lines to discourage him, but not enough to hurt him, just enough to bring him to the reality, responsibility and importance of owning and taking care of a pet.

"I know dad," replied Ralph. "I would do everything . . . . wash him, feed him, groom him, sleep with him . . . . everything. Whatever I don't know I can learn. That would be the only time I need your help, if there was something I don't know how to do."

Ralph's dad was really impressed with his son's answer, but he didn't want to show it just yet.

"Okay, he says he's going to do all these things," thought Mr. Eltison. "But is he really going to do all these things?"

Mr. Eltison wiped his mouth with his napkin.

"So you really would take care of a dog, huh?" asked Ralph's dad.

He hadn't seen his boy that excited or happy for a long time. Maybe that was what Ralph needed.

"I'll see what I can do," stated Mr. Eltison. "But no promises, okay?"

The gleam in Ralph's eyes was blinding. Happiness was a dog. The answer to loneliness and sadness was a dog, and Mr. Eltison knew it.

After Ralph went to bed that night, Mr. Eltison read the paper and relaxed for a few moments watching television. He glanced up at the clock and noticed it was getting late. He sat up and was on his way to his bedroom, but stepped into his office instead. He turned his computer on and clicked onto the page he needed. The information typed in blue reflected off of his glasses. He reached for a pen and a piece of paper. He read the writing to himself.

"Drexel's Pet Store, Main Street, open from nine til six," he said.

He jotted down the phone number and address onto the piece of paper. He shut the computer off and pulled out his daily planner. In the space for his next day's agenda, Mr. Eltison added one more line . . . . VISIT DREXEL'S PET STORE.

CHAPTER 2

IF YOU COULD IMAGINE A perfect place to live, to grow up in, and to raise a family, then you'd probably imagine a town like Spring Valley. Surrounded by mountains and nestled in a valley of gorgeous foliage, the town's name originated from the beautiful spring blossoms that just made the place look like a work of art; a masterpiece.

Spring Valley wasn't a big town at all. Anyone who moved there stayed there. Once they saw how pleasant it was to live in paradise, they settled down, found work, and raised a family.

Ralph's mom and dad grew up and lived in Spring Valley. When Paul Eltison went out on a first date with Lisa Hopkins, they both drank milkshakes at the local drug store soda fountain (White's) and finished the evening with a movie at the Palace Theatre. Four years later, just after they both finished school at the local college, Paul and Lisa married at their church in downtown Spring Valley.

Spring Valley boasted scenic views and panoramic settings. There were scores and scores of beautiful trees; maples, oaks, pines, walnuts, and many more varieties. In the spring, there were many wonderful, colorful buds, and in the fall the collection of colorful leaves before they fell just made folks stop and take a mental picture of the amazing view in front of them.

Other than the trees outlining the mountains that surrounded the valley, a great deal of the town's trees were discovered at the Spring Valley Park. The park housed a very big lake, where folks could boat, fish, and swim. There was a pool, an abundance of picnic areas, nature trails, baseball and soccer fields, and playgrounds for the citizens to enjoy. Spring Valley would host celebrations for holidays such as Memorial Day and Independence Day at the park.

The park was situated close to the town's main hub; downtown Spring Valley. Not too far from the Valleydale subdivision where Ralph and his dad lived, one could travel downtown, with a quick drive, walk, or ride down Pleasant Grove Road. To the left for over a mile, was Spring Valley Park. To get to Main Street and downtown, one would have to take a right off Pleasant Grove Road.

There were many businesses and attractive structures downtown. With the exception of a real supermarket and gas station, downtown basically had everything folks needed. People could eat, watch a flick, go shopping, and get their banking needs completed downtown.

When turning onto Main Street, the first building on the right was Jessup's. It was a men's tailoring shop. The men of Spring Valley could get their favorite suits tailored. Mr. Jessup would also alter ladies dresses and outfits.

Next to Jessup's on the right was Gletzky's Department Store. Gletzky's had everything folks needed; from clothes to toys, tools to furniture, and even some groceries. Whatever the season, Mr. Gletzky always decorated his storefront with the latest gadgets and goodies for all to see and purchase.

To the right of Gletzky's was White's Drug Store. Along with providing the medicine needed for Spring Valley, Mr. and Mrs. White boasted the town's only soda fountain. The best burgers, fries, and milkshakes were served at the soda fountain.

The Towne Bakery Shoppe baked the finest breads and pastries. Folks could tell by the heavenly aroma when the shop was baking its goods, which was basically most of the day.

Next to the bakery was the Spring Valley National Bank, Spring Valley's largest bank. Mrs. Simon was the bank manager. If folks needed money to buy a house or car, they usually visited Mrs. Simon at the bank.

Main Street crossed with First Street where the bank was. If you kept moving forward down Main Street past First Street, you ended up at the Spring Valley Train Station. Every day the citizens of Spring Valley knew when the trains were arriving and departing, for they heard the steam whistles of the train engine as it was coming and going.

On one side of First Street—which crossed with Main Street—was the police department, city hall, fire station, and hospital. Across the street from the hospital was the Spring Valley Public Library.

The police department was very small. Sheriff Thomas and Deputy Taylor basically ran the police station. There was no real crime in the town, for folks in Spring Valley were very honest and trustworthy. Responding to traffic accidents and helping citizens were the main duties for the officers of the police department.

The mayor of Spring Valley, Mayor Helms, worked out of the city hall building. Folks would find him walking either along Main or First Streets, greeting folks with kind words and a handshake.

The post office, Brady's Barber Shop, and an office structure lined the other side of First Street. Wendy Rodgers, Jenny's mom, worked out of one of the offices in that building. Brady's was the best place for men young and old to get an affordable shave and haircut.

First Street led way to Maple Avenue. Maple Avenue was named for its gorgeous maple trees, which lined each side of the avenue. When autumn was in full swing, Maple Avenue was filled with bright reds, yellows, and oranges. Ralph's church was located on Maple Avenue, as well as Betty's Boutique, the Herald Newspaper, and Hargrove's Ladies Wear.

Across from the Spring Valley National Bank on Main Street was Feldman's Hardware Store. Mr. Feldman carried all kinds of tools, lumber, garden seeds, paint, snow blowers, and lawn mowers. If you needed any type of screw or nail, Mr. Feldman had it in his store.

The next building just past Feldman's was the Palace Theatre. The Palace played the most popular movies, plus would have double features on the weekends. When walking down Main Street, if you couldn't smell the fresh breads from the bakery, you would definitely get a whiff of freshly popped popcorn. The theatre opened up its balcony on the weekends, when there were more customers coming to watch the movies.

Brown's Restaurant was situated on the other side of the Palace. Brown's was the town's favorite restaurant. The Brown's prepared a variety of foods that met the customer's needs. Ralph and his dad ate at Brown's almost every Friday night.

The last store on Main Street was Drexel's Pet Store. Mr. Drexel stocked anything and everything for dogs, cats, fish, hamsters, turtles, birds, rabbits, ferrets, snakes, and spiders. He usually had a dog or two that he kept in the storefront window display to entice future owners to come in and pet the puppies.

It was the day after Ralph had brought up the subject of wanting a dog to his dad. Mr. Eltison took a break from his work around lunchtime and drove over to Drexel's. When he arrived at the store, he noticed no puppies in the window, but the other window displayed two pouncing kittens, playing with a toy mouse.

Mr. Drexel was cleaning out a bird cage when he caught a glimpse of Mr. Eltison strolling through the dog supply aisle.

"You looking for something for your dog?" asked Mr. Drexel.

"Actually, thinking about getting a dog for my son's birthday," returned Mr. Eltison.

Mr. Drexel scratched his head and thought for a few seconds.

"Mr. Eltison right . . . . that's right, I remember you," stated Mr. Drexel. "You were thinking about getting a dog, right?"

Mr. Eltison nodded. He didn't want to tell the pet store owner the reason he never did, but folks in Spring Valley pretty much knew each other, so Mr. Drexel probably figured out why the Eltisons never purchased a dog.

"I didn't see any dogs in your window," said Mr. Eltison. "Do you have any or know when some may be coming in?"

"Well, we had one here for a couple of weeks, a real cute Cocker Spaniel," returned Mr. Drexel. "Lady and her daughter came and bought her last night just around dinner time. You probably know her . . . . lives in your neighborhood. Mrs. Rod . . . . Rodgers. Yes, that's her name."

Mr. Eltison nodded and rubbed his chin for a few seconds.

"My son's birthday is coming up next week," said Mr. Eltison. "You think you might have some more dogs soon?"

"I suppose," answered Mr. Drexel. "Never really know when they're gonna bring them. Half the time I don't get any. What size you looking at for a dog?"

"Something not too big, but not too small," answered Mr. Eltison as he chuckled.

Mr. Drexel knew exactly what he meant. Even though Jenny's mom had bought the last dog the night before, Mr. Eltison wasn't sure that a Cocker Spaniel was what Ralph wanted, so he wasn't too upset (although Ralph would be happy with any dog). He was concerned that there might not be any dogs arriving before Ralph's birthday.

"Take a look in the paper," mentioned Mr. Drexel. "Sometimes folks give away free puppies. I'll call you as soon as one comes in."

With that last exchange of conversation, Ralph's dad wrote down his number and handed it to the pet store owner. Mr. Drexel went back to work and Mr. Eltison headed over to Brown's for some lunch. Brown's food was just too good to be so close and not stop in, so he picked up a bite to eat before he headed home.

Ralph hadn't mentioned anything about a new dog in the neighborhood. Jenny liked Ralph as a friend, but they didn't hang out much, so Ralph probably didn't know that Jenny was getting a dog. Between that day and Ralph's birthday, Mr. Eltison had to come up with a plan. If Mr. Drexel didn't have a dog in time for Ralph's birthday, Mr. Eltison was going to have to get one from somewhere else.

CHAPTER 3

THE NAME WALTER EUGENE CRUM didn't sound too mean or intimidating. It was rare indeed, but not scary at all. So why did folks tremble at the sound of his name? Well, certain folks did, just not those from Spring Valley anyhow.

About forty miles north of Spring Valley, over the mountains, was the closest town tucked halfway up another set of mountains. Bordertown was its name, because it was in fact located on the border of the state, very close to its neighboring state.

Bordertown was nothing like Spring Valley. Sure, folks lived there. They worked, they lived in houses, but it was quite different. There was no park for kids and adults to play in. There were no swimming pools, but there was a muddy lake that citizens swam in. Yuck!

Bordertown was lined with many factories. Smoke billowed from the smokestacks constantly. There were coal yards, a coal mine, and even a giant rock quarry. There were forests, but workers continuously cut down trees to use for the factories, so trees had become less visible.

The town originated from the coal mines many years ago, and used to be a thriving one. Workers who spent many years in the mines and yards raised their families and wanted to live in their town. That changed about thirty years ago.

A young man named Walter Eugene Crum grew up in Bordertown. When he was a baby, Crum was left at the doorsteps of an orphanage. No one knew where he came from or who his parents were. He was never adopted. He went to school, and then received a scholarship to go to college out of state. He vowed to return after college and start a family. He searched long and hard for his parents, but every clue led to a dead end.

Walter did return to Bordertown and became the youngest bank manager ever at Bordertown Savings and Trust in downtown Bordertown. He had this grandiose idea of wanting to run the entire town; to make it his own.

Walter never found a wife and therefore, he never had any children. He made very good money and became one of the richest men in town from not only his position at the bank, but from making very wise business decisions. Within twenty years, Walter became the owner of the bank, he opened and owned five factories, and owned about fifty percent of the town's real estate.

You would think that being rich would make a person happy, but not Crum. Through all of his years working, he still couldn't find his parents. He wanted to show them that they had made a mistake in dropping him off at the orphanage; that they needed to see what a success he was. But as the years passed, Crum became more bitter and sour. No one would marry him, not even for his money, for he was so heartless.

Being the owner of the bank meant he controlled who would get money and who would not. He would charge very high interest on those he did approve, and made triple the money that the person borrowed by the time the loan was paid back.

For many years Crum became the mayor, too. That position gave him more power. Even though he wasn't liked, he controlled the money in Bordertown. So if folks didn't want their rent or taxes raised, they had to vote for Crum.

Walter Crum was very shrewd with his money. He would only spend money to acquire things, and usually spent next to nothing afterwards to keep things running. So houses, factories, and apartments were run down, and he kept raising the rent on folks.

And as the years passed, Walter E. Crum despised seeing people happy, so he made it his personal mission for the citizens of Bordertown to be miserable. He ordered all swimming pools and playgrounds to be replaced by some kind of factory or building. Soon there was no place to have fun. The only fun kids had were bicycles, because Crum owned a bicycle shop and folks had to pay him in order to purchase one.

Within the thirty years of Crum's return to Bordertown, he owned almost everything in Bordertown. If folks wanted to buy a house, car, groceries, get a job . . . . you name it, Walter Eugene Crum had something to do with it.

Citizens of Bordertown had not only to pay Crum for rent and taxes, but protection services and other fees to keep their businesses from going out of business. Only one person kept the businesses going in Bordertown and his name was Walter Eugene Crum.

Crum didn't spend much money on his appearance. Growing up in an orphanage, Walter was used to not owning many clothes. Even though he had the money to purchase any style of attire that he desired, Crum kept his appearance simple. He wore a black suit, white shirt, black tie and shoes, plus a black top hat. He only owned two suits, and they were exactly the same. He would just simply wear the black suit while the other one was being cleaned.

Crum hired five thugs to collect money and enforce his shrewd laws on is citizens. He paid them very little, but the men didn't care, for they were working for the most important man in town.

These men were big, and not pretty to look at. They dressed in black, hardly ever shaved, and probably never bathed either.

All of the men possessed very mean and intimidating names. The leader was named Frake. Joining him was his brother Jake, and three other henchmen named Sid, Bull, and Jeb. If any of these five men entered into an establishment or home, whatever they asked for, folks handed over.

So why not move out of Bordertown? A few escaped, but went far away, never to be found; afraid that Crum's men would come after them. The problem was not many folks were moving in, so the town started suffering, for Crum had all the money and the residents had none.

One early October morning, Crum called a meeting to address that very problem. The men walked through the bank lobby and straight into Crum's office. They all sat down while the old man wrote numbers into a huge ledger that he kept on his desk. He uttered numbers and figures to himself before Frake cleared his throat. Crum looked up and noticed his five men before him. He threw down his pencil and rested his spectacles on the desk.

"You wanted to see us Mr. Crum," said Frake.

Crum shifted his beady eyes at every man, then picked his glasses and rested them on the bridge of his nose.

"So what do you have for me this morning?" asked Crum. "I'm assuming you finished your collections for the week."

Crum rubbed his wrinkled hands together, for he anticipated a big stack of cash on his desk.

Each man slowly pulled out a small roll of money from their pockets and hesitantly placed the rolls on Crum's desk. Crum gazed at the little pile, and then sternly stared at each man.

"So it's come to this, huh?" asked Crum.

"Mr. Crum, folks don't have more money to give," answered Frake. "We've taken all they have. They can't even pay the rent."

"So kick them out!" blasted Crum.

"There's no one else to take their place sir," returned Frake. "It's better to get something instead of nothing."

Crum continued to stare at the money, and then at the men.

"So what can we do to improve our situation?" asked Crum.

Crum had all the money he needed and more, but had become a shrewd and greedy man. Certainly he would never spend the money he had, even if he lived to two-hundred. He owned a giant house, but usually only lived out of one or two rooms. With the exception of Frake and Sid (Sid usually drove Mr. Crum to and from home), no one was ever invited to his house. Crum employed a butler and a maid, but didn't pay them. He felt that living in his house for free was their payment.

Frake and his men looked at each other. They sat silent for a moment. With the exception of Frake, Crum's henchmen were not very smart, but they followed orders really well. Frake thought of an idea.

"Sir, you own basically everything in Bordertown, and you want more, correct?" asked Frake.

Crum displayed a devilish smile. His eyes burned with earnest, waiting for Frake to continue.

"Go on man!" blasted Crum.

"You need to expand your empire sir," returned Frake. "Continue running Bordertown, but expand to the next town and transform it into your town."

Crum wheeled his chair around to a map on his wall of Bordertown and the surrounding areas. He rose to examine it carefully. He followed his crinkled finger as it moved down from Bordertown to its closest neighbor . . . . Spring Valley.

"Spring Valley, I've always despised that name," said Crum. "Sounds too happy and joyful, it needs to be more depressing and glum."

"Exactly sir," said Frake. "You're a genius sir."

"And you have a plan?" inquired Crum.

"I think I do," responded Frake.

The other four men smiled, they knew Crum was delighted with the thought of making more money.

"How much do we need for an initial investment?" asked Crum.

"Not too much," answered Frake. "We'll make the townsfolk pay for their own downfall."

"I think I know where you're going with this," smirked Crum as he rubbed his hands together and chuckled lightly. "We have some planning to do, don't we my good man?"

Frake nodded in agreement. Crum pushed a button on his phone to contact his secretary.

"Hold all my calls until further notice!" commanded Crum. "We will be in a meeting for most of the day."

Frake rose and moved his chair closer to his boss. The other men converged behind Frake, eager to catch a glimpse of his evil plan.

Life changed for the residents of Spring Valley that day, even though nothing would happen for awhile. A plan was being set to destroy the beautiful town of Spring Valley and turn it into another Bordertown. The worst thing was that no one from Spring Valley expected it. Life was so good there. There was never cause for concern. Walter E. Crum was about to take a bite out of Spring Valley, and the town didn't even know that it was on his menu.

CHAPTER 4

JENNY RODGERS DIDN'T TALK TO Ralph Eltison that much, in or out of school. She did like him, as a friend that was, but there wasn't a true friendship, not yet. She walked home with him from school sometimes, but most of the time Ralph left before her, for he wanted to spend as much time as he could visiting the neighborhood dogs.

So during lunch time on a school day in early October, Jenny passed by Ralph, who usually sat alone at a table that was situated in the corner of the cafeteria.

"Hey Ralph, do you mind if I sit beside you?" asked Jenny.

Ralph shook his head no and scooted his chair over for Jenny to fit beside him. She pulled out her lunch and took a bite of her sandwich, and then swallowed her food.

"I see you stop by to pet the dogs in our neighborhood," said Jenny. "I wanted to know if you wanted to pet my dog?"

Ralph stopped eating his sandwich.

"I didn't know you had a dog," answered Ralph.

"Just got her the other day," said Jenny. "Her name is Bernadette and she's a Cocker Spaniel."

"I've seen a picture of one in a book," returned Ralph. "They're really beautiful dogs."

"Thanks," said Jenny. "If you want, I can walk home with you. Then we can stop at my house and you can meet Bernadette."

"Thanks," said Ralph, and they agreed to meet each other after school.

"I asked for a dog for my birthday," said Ralph. "Maybe if I get one, you can come and meet my dog."

"That would be awesome," said Jenny as she walked off, threw her lunch stuff away, and then headed to the line to go back to class.

Ralph thought for a moment. Not only was that the nicest thing a kid had ever done; coming over and talking to him that is. But asking him to walk with her and letting him meet her new dog; now that was downright nice, too. Ralph was excited about meeting Jenny's dog, Bernadette. And he was excited about walking home with Jenny Rodgers, a girl who had always smiled when he passed by or said kind words to him.

What made Ralph more hyped was the thought of him walking his dog while Jenny walked her dog. His birthday was in less than a week, and his dad had not mentioned anything to him in response to Ralph's birthday request a few nights before. He wondered if his dad had any luck finding him a dog. How big would it be? His mind began to wander. Before Ralph knew it, Mrs. Randolph had to remind him to throw his garbage away and get in line.

Ralph's dad was not having much luck finding a puppy, and he was coming to the realization that Ralph might not be receiving a puppy for his birthday. Maybe it would be Christmas instead. Mr. Eltison had scanned the local paper, and even local websites on the computer. For whatever reason, maybe it was just that time of the year; there were no puppies for sale in Spring Valley. But fate was in the favor of the Eltisons that night.

Mr. Drexel was closing up his pet store that evening. The sign on his door stated that his pet store was open on weeknights from nine in the morning until six o'clock at night. Most of the time Mr. Drexel would keep his doors open until seven, for he would finish any work he had that day and figured if he was staying late, he might as well keep the doors open and generate a few extra sales.

Darkness approached around seven o'clock. Mr. Drexel locked his front doors, placed all of his cash and credit card receipts in a bank bag, and headed to his office, which was situated at the back of the store. While he was counting his money and placing it in his safe, Mr. Drexel heard a strange noise coming from behind the building. He had heard that noise many times before in his life, but knew it couldn't be that noise, not in his back alley. He grabbed a flashlight from his desk drawer and proceeded to the back door.

Mr. Drexel opened the back door slowly. The only light in the alley near his building was a light pole that lit up half of his part and half of his neighbor Brown's half of the back alley. He continued to hear the noise; a sound like whimpering and crying, but not from a baby. It was a definitely an animal.

The pet store owner walked outside and slowly peeked to his left. He saw nothing. Then he looked to his right. All he saw was the dumpster. Then he heard the whimpering noise again. The noise was definitely originating from behind the dumpster.

Mr. Drexel turned his flashlight on and shined it behind the dumpster. He found the source of the whimpering noises, cuddled up against the wall, next to an old piece of cardboard and some newspaper.

"What in the world are you doing here?" asked Mr. Drexel. "Where did you come from?"

Mr. Drexel bent down to take a closer look. He still couldn't believe what he saw. Still wedged up against the wall was a puppy. He was a little less than a foot long. When Mr. Drexel placed his hand on the puppy, all it did was shiver a bit, it was cool outside, and for some reason, the puppy was wet.

Mr. Drexel picked up the pup and took it inside. He wiped the puppy down with a towel. He examined its underside and determined that it was a boy. There were no dog tags, and he checked for a chip locator device in the young dog.

The pet store owner stepped back and examined his discovery. The pup was black and brown all over, except for a few white spots; one on his tail, another on his belly and chest, and a couple on his legs.

"Maybe a labrador with a little collie mixed in," said Mr. Drexel as he continued his examination.

After a quick grooming, Mr. Drexel placed the puppy in a cage. He brought some food and water and placed the bowls in the cage. The puppy wasted no time, he was very hungry and thirsty. He also seemed very happy to have been found, as he was eating, the pup's tail wagged vigorously.

Mr. Drexel watched the puppy eat for a few minutes, then went back to his desk and finished his paperwork. He then reached for a piece of paper and grabbed his phone.

"Yes, is this Mr. Eltison?" asked Mr. Drexel. "Drexel here. Listen, you still looking for a pup?"

Mr. Drexel paused for a few seconds as he awaited Mr. Eltison's response.

"Well, I might have something for you," continued Mr. Drexel. "Why don't you stop by tomorrow."

After the phone call, Mr. Drexel checked on the puppy one more time. He then turned off the lights and left via the back door.

Like a kid who anticipated Christmas, Mr. Eltison couldn't wait until the next day to come. Although he knew owning a dog would be a gigantic change in both his and Ralph's lives, he knew that a pet was what they both needed, a loving animal that would bring happiness to both of their lives, especially his boy's, who was having a tough time coping with the absence of his mother. He tossed and turned, and waited for morning to arrive.

When morning did come, it was tough for Mr. Eltison to wake up, for he lost many hours of sleep, and he did have a very busy work day ahead. He woke Ralph, prepared his breakfast and school lunch, and made sure he was ready to head out for school on time. Ralph's dad stayed busy until eleven o'clock, but then took a break from his work to take care of that very important matter; Ralph's birthday present.

When Mr. Eltison arrived at Drexel's, he walked straight over to the dog cages, which were empty except for one. There was a green "SOLD" sign affixed to the one cage that housed a puppy. Mr. Eltison wondered if Mr. Drexel had already sold the dog earlier, or was the pet store owner confident that Mr. Eltison would indeed purchase the pup. He peeked inside and glanced at the puppy. Curled up in a little ball was a mix of black, brown, and specks of white, his hair still scruffy from being wet the night before.

"He's a mutt all right," came a voice from behind Mr. Eltison.

Mr. Eltison turned around to find the pet store owner with a clipboard and price labeler in his hand.

"Has he been sold already?" asked Ralph's dad.

"Sure," answered Mr. Drexel. "You're buying him, right?"

Mr. Eltison breathed a sigh of relief.

"When did you get him?" asked Mr. Eltison.

"Well, he kind of showed up last night" replied Mr. Drexel. "I think he came knowing that someone really wanted a puppy."

Mr. Eltison continued to stare at the puppy, who had just woken up, and made his way to the front of the cage. The pup started to wag his tail and stretch.

"He is adorable," said Ralph's dad. "How big will he get?"

Mr. Drexel scratched his head for a few seconds.

"I figure about sixty pounds, if you keep him exercised, but don't hold me to that number," replied a chuckling Mr. Drexel.

"He's just what we wanted," said an enthusiastic Mr. Eltison. "How much for him?"

"Well, since he came to me as a gift, I figure I just hand him over to you," said Mr. Drexel.

"Wow, really?" asked Mr. Eltison.

Mr. Drexel smiled.

"I'll make enough selling all the things he'll need," answered Mr. Drexel.

Mr. Drexel ushered the new pet owner over to dog supply aisle. He pushed a wheeled cart over to Mr. Eltison. He handed Ralph's dad a pet carrier, a food dish, water bowl, wet and dry puppy food, a grooming brush, some doggie treats, a doggie bed, a leash, a red collar, and all the flea and tick medicine needed to keep those pesky insects out of the house. Mr. Drexel also grabbed about five different types of toys for the pup, including a chew-toy, a tug-of-war sock, and a big red bouncy ball.

"Is he going to be spending a great deal of time outside?" asked Mr. Drexel.

"I suppose so," answered Mr. Eltison.

"Then I recommend one of these," commented Mr. Drexel. "They're pretty easy to install."

Mr. Drexel handed Mr. Eltison a doggie door with a flap, which after installed would allow the dog to enter and exit without needing a human to let him out. Mr. Drexel showed Ralph's dad a doghouse, which Mr. Eltison also agreed to purchase.

By the time Mr. Eltison walked out with his son's new puppy, he displayed an overflowing cart full of supplies and a doghouse. His new challenge was where he was going to hide all of this stuff, including a new puppy? Ralph's birthday was still a couple of days away. He thought he might just have to present Ralph the pup a couple of days early.

"We'll see how it goes," said Mr. Eltison to himself.

Ralph's dad opened the garage door and brought the puppy and supplies inside. The puppy carrier had a place to put newspaper inside to catch the puppy's droppings, and there was enough room to use small dishes for food and water. The big challenge was how to keep the puppy quiet, for he was sure as soon as he left the room, the puppy would begin to yelp. And he was correct.

"Why should I make Ralph wait two more days and put all this stress on this poor puppy?" thought Mr. Eltison to himself.

It was decided, after an early dinner, Ralph was going to get the surprise of his life.

When Ralph returned home from school, it was a little later than normal as he did walk home with Jenny Rodgers. He and Jenny stopped by Juan's, Sarge's and Max's house before they went back to Jenny's house to play with Bernadette.

Jenny's puppy was very small too. She was reddish-brown with floppy ears. In just a few short days, Bernadette had learned the run of the house, including where the food bowl was, and she was potty-trained to do her business outside. Mrs. Rodgers left Bernadette outside to play in the fenced-in yard while she and Jenny were gone, but the puppy stayed inside most of the day when they came home.

Ralph loved petting and playing with Bernadette. Jenny could see the excitement in his eyes and smile on his face while he was playing with her pup. Bernadette liked playing with Ralph, but was already in love with her Jenny. The pup followed her human around everywhere.

Ralph thanked Jenny for the visit and then headed home. While he was gone, the new puppy had grown quite vocal, he wanted someone to keep him company in the garage. He yelped and yelped, but finally grew tired and took a nap just minutes before Ralph came home.

Mr. Eltison tried to keep Ralph busy with some outside chores and made sure he didn't go near the garage. Ralph also had some homework to finish. By the time he finished, Ralph's dad was calling him for dinner.

"Well, we're probably going out to eat on your birthday," said Ralph's dad. "So tonight, I'm going to fix your favorite . . . . cheeseburgers and French fries. And I have a little surprise for you after dinner."

Ralph enjoyed the dinner, but couldn't wait for the surprise. What could it be? Where was the surprise? Would they have to go somewhere to find the surprise?

"If you help me get the dishes done, we can go see your surprise," said Ralph's dad.

Ralph eagerly agreed to help his dad. After the last dish was dried, Ralph's dad asked Ralph to stay in the kitchen and he excused himself, stating he would be back in a few minutes with his surprise.

Ralph's dad returned to the kitchen with a piece of red cloth in his hand. He motioned for Ralph to come on over. He tied the cloth around Ralph's forehead and covered his eyes, making a blindfold. Ralph's dad led Ralph into the garage.

"Happy birthday son," Ralph's dad said as he lifted the blindfold from Ralph's eyes.

Ralph could not believe what he saw. In the middle of the garage floor was the pet carrier with a big red bow on it. Inside the carrier, Ralph saw the most amazing black, brown and white puppy.

At first Ralph was speechless and then his emotions caught up with him. "Oh wow!" exclaimed Ralph. "Thanks dad!"

Ralph's dad smiled, patted Ralph on the shoulder, and motioned for him to bend down. Ralph opened the carrier door and the puppy came running out with his tail wagging. The puppy immediately jumped into Ralph's lap and covered his face with dog kisses.

"He's so awesome!" yelled Ralph as the pup continued to lick and wag.

"He's going to be a big responsibility," said Ralph's dad as he watched Ralph receive a multitude of kisses from the puppy. "We've got to get this one potty-trained before we can let him have free range of the house."

"I'll do whatever it takes," Ralph said excitedly.

Together Ralph and his dad played with the puppy. They took the puppy outside and let him run around the fenced-in yard, but he stayed close to the house and garage. They did get the puppy to do his business outside, which was a good start in the potty-training process.

When they returned inside, Ralph's dad laid out the doggie bed next to the cage. They set the food and water dishes next to the doggie bed. Ralph's dad placed some newspapers out on the garage floor just in case the puppy couldn't hold his business overnight.

"Is it a boy or a girl?" asked Ralph.

"A boy," answered Ralph's dad. "What are you going to name him?"

"I don't know," Ralph said. He was petting his puppy and rolling the red ball for the puppy to chase.

"Can he sleep with me tonight?" asked Ralph.

"Let's get him used to things here first," replied Mr. Eltison. "He'll be sleeping in your room before you know it."

So Ralph bathed while the puppy rested. The boy wasn't going to get much sleep that night, he was just too excited. After his bath, Ralph went back to the garage to be with his birthday present and had to be told numerous times by his father that he had to get to bed.

Ralph couldn't believe it. His wish had come true. He got what he wanted for his birthday. Now he was going to enjoy his gift every minute of every day of his life. After he left the puppy, Ralph kept hearing him yelp. Ralph wanted to go back to the garage, but his dad reminded him that he had school in the morning. The puppy was going to be fine. All puppies yelp when they first get to a new place and they have to get used to their new homes. While it was a struggle, Ralph finally fell asleep.

When he woke up in the morning, Ralph took his pup out and let him take care of his business. He fed him and made sure he had plenty of water. He then played with the pup before he had to eat breakfast and head out for school.

Ralph met Jenny at her house and told her his exciting news. She too was excited. He and Jenny played with Bernadette before they left, and the two of them walked to school.

Jenny agreed to walk home with Ralph after school. Their plan was to stop at her house, pet Bernadette, and then walk to Ralph's house to meet his new pup.

In school, Ralph could hardly keep focused. Instead of daydreaming about Mr. Magnificent, Ralph thought about his puppy. He did manage to keep himself focused enough not to cause a disturbance in class. The wait was going to be tough. All he wanted was to get home and play with his birthday gift.

School couldn't end fast enough, but when it did, Ralph and Jenny raced home to be with their dogs. They didn't bother visiting the other dogs in the neighborhood that day. They both had their own dogs to visit now. Ralph was sure he would visit the dogs and cat again. It was just now he had his own dog to take care of.

When they arrived at Jenny's house, Jenny and Ralph played and pet Bernadette for a while.

"I have an idea," said Jenny as she headed up her back porch steps and inside the house. She came back with Bernadette's leash. "We are going to have Bernadette meet your new dog, and maybe they'll become friends real fast," said an excited Jenny.

"Cool," said Ralph.

So Ralph and Jenny walked Bernadette over to Ralph's house. Jenny did a fantastic job walking her new puppy.

When they arrived at Ralph's house, Ralph told his dad that he was going to take the dog outside to play. Ralph's dad reminded him to be careful and make sure the puppy didn't get out of the fenced yard.

"He's so cute," said Jenny as she bent down to pet Ralph's puppy.

Bernadette was happy to see a new friend. Both puppies wagged their tails and eagerly sniffed each other. Then they both chased after the red ball. Both of their mouths were too small to bite into the ball and carry it around. So, the pups just nudged the ball with their noses.

"What's his name?" asked Jenny.

Ralph shook his head.

"You know, I'm not sure yet," answered Ralph. "I want it to be very special, so I'm taking my time, but he'll have one soon enough. I thought about Brownie, Blackie, or Spot."

"Those are all great names," said Jenny as she continued to pet both dogs. "Do you think that we can start walking our dogs together after school, like around the neighborhood? I'm sure my mom and your dad would be okay with it."

So Ralph asked his dad who said it would be fine, but to also check with Jenny's mom.

"Just be careful not to let your puppies free out on the road," said Mr. Eltison. "Jenny, I'll check with your mom tonight and soon you two should be out walking your dogs."

The next day brought more adventure. Not only was it Ralph's actual birthday, but after school Ralph and his dad had an appointment at the veterinarian's office. Ralph's puppy received all the shots that he needed and became a legal "dog citizen" of the town of Spring Valley. When it was time for the vet to write the puppy's name on his license, Ralph hesitated and told him he didn't have a name yet, so they just put "Eltison" on both the license and tag.

After he was finished with the appointment, Ralph and Jenny took their dogs out for their first official walk together. They all had a blast! They walked from Jenny's house on Valleydale Drive toward Schoolhouse Road and over to Ralph's house. That was quite a bit of walking for two little puppies.

The walk caught the attention of the neighborhood pets, for all the dogs (except Max) and Jasmine the cat caught glimpses of the two new puppies living in the neighborhood. Juan took a sniff of the two puppies while Sarge stood his ground and just stared at the pups.

Ralph and his dad spent the rest of his birthday night going to dinner at Brown's Family Restaurant. Ralph ordered one of their tasty cheeseburgers while his dad ordered a steak and a baked potato. After dinner, they went home and each ate a piece of the chocolate birthday cake that Mr. Eltison had baked earlier that day.

Mr. Eltison knew that he had made the right choice in giving Ralph the puppy for his birthday. Ralph had really impressed his father by taking on the responsibility of taking care of his pet right from the start.

Ralph really loved his pup. His dad let his pup sleep with Ralph on his birthday night. Luckily it was a Friday, so Ralph was able to stay up later than normal.

After his pup fell asleep, Ralph rested in bed and thought about the name of his puppy. He thought long and hard.

"I want it to be original, like no other," said Ralph to himself.

The names he had thought of earlier were not so original, he really wanted something different, something new. Then a thought came to him. He remembered what was on his puppy's tag from that afternoon . . . . "Eltison." How could he get a good name out of his last name?

Ralph soon fell asleep, but in a dream he heard himself calling for his puppy. The name he used was . . . . Elt, which was short for Eltison. It made perfect sense. It was original; no one else he knew of had a pet with that name. Plus, it sounded like a boy's name.

Ralph woke up to his puppy licking him all over his face. Ralph started laughing. He got up quickly, threw on a pair of pants and ran out the door with his pup following closely.

It was decided, "Elt" was going to be his name. It was like no other. No one had a name like that.

Ralph was excited. He ran to the backyard, Elt following Ralph like a shadow. Ralph's father was out back weeding a flower bed. He watched Ralph and his puppy scurry to the shed. Ralph came out with a can of paint and a small paint brush.

"What are you doing?" asked Ralph's dad.

Ralph set the paint can down in front of the doghouse.

"I'm going to paint his name on the top of his doghouse!" exclaimed Ralph.

"Well, what's his name?" asked his dad.

"It's a surprise, wait and see!" answered Ralph.

Ralph opened the can of red paint and proceeded to paint his new dog's name above the doorway of the doghouse. He painted . . . . "E L T."

CHAPTER 5

TIME HAD PASSED BY QUICKLY for Ralph and Elt. Every day after school, Ralph would take Elt for a walk, meeting Jenny Rodgers and Bernadette at the street corner of Springhaven Court and Valleydale Drive. Not only were Jenny and Ralph enjoying their time together during these walks, but Elt and Bernadette were hitting it off well, too. They kept pace with each other as their humans would stroll down the street.

The usual route would take them up Valleydale Drive and back, circling past Spring Drive, then to Springhaven Court, past Ralph's house, and then back to the corner where they met. Sometimes, they would walk all the way to the school on Schoolhouse Road and back. Sometimes Jenny and Ralph would go backwards, starting on Springhaven and finishing at Ralph's house.

Now their daily walks always took them past the neighborhood dogs that Ralph had visited almost every day. Ralph would make a point to stop by and see his old friends on the way home from school, but some visits were shorter, or there were times that Ralph would walk and just pass by. Ralph now had his own dog that he was responsible for. He wanted to spend time with Elt (and Bernadette).

Of course walking with Jenny had a little something to do with spending time with Bernadette.

The older dogs in the neighborhood were keeping tabs on Elt and Bernadette. They weren't too keen on having these two "newbies" walking through their neighborhood. It was a territorial kind of thing.

Now it seemed on one Wednesday per month, for no other reason than it was a time that all of their humans weren't home, the dogs of the Valleydale subdivision would meet. Yes, dogs have meetings too.

The popular spot for their meetings was an old tool shed in Sarge's yard. The meetings weren't very long, as the dogs could not be missing from home for long periods of time without being noticed.

How did the dogs flee from their homes and yards to attend the meetings? Juan's route was pretty easy. He had dug a hole that was under both a bush and his fence. He simply squirmed his way under the fence, and scurried past one house and "ta-da," there he was, in the back of the tool shed, which was conveniently nestled against the back fence. There was even a hole dug under the fence behind the tool shed.

Max, getting up there in the age department, was in no mood to dig and burrow his way through a hole. Besides, he was too big to fit in one of those holes. Max's talent was the way he could maneuver the front gate latch. Getting out of his gate was a cinch, but crossing the street and nudging Sarge's gate was a challenge. He knew though, about an hour or so before the meeting time that Sarge the Boxer would charge over to his gate, lean up against it and gently adjust the clamp, making it easier for Max to open it.

Max wouldn't always make it to every meeting. He would blame his "getting up in years" as an excuse for his absence. When they didn't understand, or in Sarge's case, was too upset for reason, Max would remind them that he was the first pet in the neighborhood. He had been there long before any of them and he was the senior member of the group. He was holding meetings with other dogs long before any of the others had moved into the neighborhood.

There was always a mystery surrounding Chin and how he arrived to the dog meetings. He would show up without anyone noticing him enter, stay quiet for most of the meeting, and then usually end the meeting with one of his famous proverbs. Most if not all the time, these proverbs had nothing to do with what the dogs were talking about.

Yes, talking. Every animal in the world communicated somehow. Dogs barked for a reason. That was their way of talking. One more thing, dogs and cats, for some weird reason, could understand each other. Maybe it was because as pets they knew one another, mostly as adversaries. Not sure why, but they did.

The old tool shed in Mr. Davis's yard was just big enough to hold these meetings. The only dog that didn't attend the meetings, other than the new ones Bernadette and Elt, was Prince.

"Royalty would never associate themselves with peasants," declared Prince as he walked past the other dogs in his neighborhood with his human, Mr. Dawkins.

A few holes in the side wall of the shed emitted just enough sunlight for each pooch to see each other. Sarge would push the shed door shut once all the dogs were present and accounted for.

"Well, I see old Max is missing another important meeting," grumbled Sarge. "Now, let's see what's on our agenda."

"Hold on you old blowhard!" blurted Max as he wedged his way into the tool shed. "You know to give me a few minutes . . . . these legs just don't get me here as fast as they used to."

Sarge rolled his eyes. The Boxer pulled out a clipboard from under a stack of papers and started pawing through the papers.

"Now, what's on our agenda?" he asked. "Oh, yeah, what are we going to do with these two little whippersnappers that walk by us every day?"

"Those two?" replied Max. "Never seen them. I'm usually indoors with the lady of the house around their walk time I guess."

"I think they're nice," said Juan, while he wagged his tail happily. "The little muchaco still stops by and visits me."

Sarge looked over at Chin, who stood at attention. He remained silent and kept his eyes closed.

"Chin, you got any thoughts on these two?" asked Sarge.

Chin said nothing. He wasn't sleeping, just in deep thought.

Sarge continued. "Does anyone know their names?"

"Elt and Bernadette, I believe," mentioned a voice from above.

The dogs, with the exception of Chin, gazed up at the tool shed ceiling. Perched above them on one of the rafters was Jasmine, Mrs. Reed's tabby cat.

"What is she doing here?" asked Sarge. Can't you see this is a dogs only meeting going on in here?"

"Oh leave her alone," squawked Max. "She always comes to these meetings and you always gripe about it. She may not be a canine, but she is part of the neighborhood."

"She's okay to me," Juan interjected.

"Everything is okay to you!" exclaimed Sarge.

The Boxer shook his paw at Jasmine. Why if you were down here I'd . . . ." Sarge barked.

"Meowwww!" purred Jasmine.

"Ooh!" complained Sarge as he stomped back and forth on the tool shed floor.

"They're very young," explained Jasmine. "I believe we were all very young once, and welcomed to the neighborhood. I think we should give the same courtesy that was given to us. Welcome them."

"I already did!" shouted Juan excitedly. "I let them sniff me the other day."

Sarge shook his head in disgust.

Then Max responded "I'd say we let 'em grow up a little, until after the snow comes, and then invite 'em to our next meeting."

"All in favor, say I," said a dejected Sarge.

The dogs, including Chin and the one cat Jasmine, all raised their right paws with approval to Max's plan. Even Sarge raised his paw after he saw everyone else doing it.

"We'll have to find a bigger meeting place," noted Jasmine. "I'd prefer something with a ledge, please."

Sarge grunted. "It would be kind of tight in here with two more bodies. I guess that's all we have for this meeting."

All of the animals then turned their attention to Chin. The meeting was over and it was time for the Chow Chow's words of wisdom. Chin's eyes opened, and all eyes were fixed upon his very next move. Then Chin spoke.

"Old Chinese proverb says two heads better than one, except when you have headache."

Chin nodded his head in approval of what he had just said. The other dogs and Jasmine looked at each other, trying to figure out what Chin's message meant. Nothing Chin had said at the end of these meetings ever made any sense, but it seemed that this time the others were more confused than ever. Sarge shook off his dazed expression long enough to ask a question.

"Okay, who wants to speak to the two pups?"

"I will, said Jasmine. "It's time they meet a feline with an attitude."

"It is done," stated Max. "Until we meet again after the snow comes."

"And we find another meeting place, maybe at me casa!" shouted a jubilant Juan.

"We'll see if those two newbies will come," commanded Sarge. "Then we'll see about changing the meeting place. This meeting is adjourned!"

The four dogs and cat went their separate ways. Sarge nudged the tool shed door shut and started back on his daily routine of guarding Mr. Davis's house and yard.

There was a final decision. The neighborhood pets were going to allow Elt and Bernadette to attend their meetings. That was an honor, if Max wanted it, and Sarge approved it, then that meant something. Elt and Bernadette were going to be officially welcomed to the neighborhood, and what better way would there be than to join their club?

Elt and Bernadette were still puppies and knew nothing about clubs, meetings, and even a cat for that matter. Jasmine would be the one inviting them. Their business was to eat, play, tear up things, and go for long walks together. Life would change for them as they grew older. The holidays were coming, and soon they would face new and exciting experiences.

CHAPTER 6

LIFE FOR RALPH AND ELT was good. The boy and his dog were enjoying life and enjoying each other. In just two weeks, Elt had nearly doubled in size. He ate, drank, slept, and played with his favorite human.

Ralph kept up after Elt. Ralph groomed him with a dog brush. The boy monitored Elt's food and water, following his dad's recommendations on how much to feed Elt. Ralph walked Elt at least once a day with Jenny Rodgers. He also played out in the yard with his pup.

School and studies had gone much smoother than ever for Ralph. Grades were improving and he was paying better attention to Mrs. Randolph. Sometimes his mind would wander, trying to figure out where he was going to walk Elt that day, but he'd quickly snap out of it and get back on task.

Although Ralph still imagined being a superhero like Mr. Magnificent and saving the world from evil-doers like Dr. Plasmo, these thoughts usually happened at night before bed. Ralph and his dad would talk about which superhero they would be at dinner, but Ralph had kept his imagination under control.

Elt really had it made. He had the "run of the house," but usually stayed away from Mr. Eltison's room and office. Ralph knew not to go there, especially if his dad was busy. Elt sensed that those areas were "no play zones," so he stayed away, too. By the time Ralph would let his dad know he was home from school, Elt had already jumped on Ralph, chewed the boy's pants cuffs, and was sitting at the back door, waiting for Ralph to take him for his daily walk.

Elt's food and water dish were in the kitchen, between a table and a counter that was near one of the two kitchen windows. Elt was fed twice a day; once in the morning, and then second at dinner time. Ralph usually fed Elt some brand of puppy dry food that his dad picked up at Drexel's Pet Store. On special occasions, Elt would receive moist food from a can. Elt preferred the moist food of course, but sometimes Ralph would have to plug his nose with his hand because the moist food was so smelly.

Playtime was mostly all the time until bedtime for Elt, he was still a puppy and that's what a puppy did. His favorite toy was the red ball that Mr. Drexel had sold to Ralph's dad. He also adored the chew-bones and the tug-of-war sock.

Doing his business was easier with the assistance of the doggie door that Ralph's dad had installed.

"That was a wise investment," Ralph's dad proudly boasted.

When Ralph's dad was out on a job, Elt could step out and not have to worry about someone letting him out. He could leave and enter at his own leisure. There was always a bird or squirrel to chase, or an occasional passerby that needed to be barked at. Elt was the protector of his home.

In the short time Elt had lived in his new home, he did manage to exhibit normal puppy behavior. In other words, Elt messed up some things. He did chew on everything in sight. He spilled water on the kitchen floor when he accidentally ran into his water dish. Even though he used the doggie door and went on walks, Elt did have a couple of isolated accidents. Once he got used to the doggie door, Elt worked hard doing his duty, and the accidents ceased. Sometimes there would be unraveled toilet paper or shredded newspaper in the hall or living room, but all in all, Elt was a very well behaved pup.

As fall arrived and the leaves fell, leaf raking and jumping into leaf piles became a favorite pastime for Ralph and Elt. Sometimes the whole leaf raking and yard cleaning project took longer than expected, but Ralph's dad remembered what it was like to be a kid, so he wasn't so hard on his son for jumping in the leaves before the clean-up was completed.

Soon all the leaves were off the trees, and what leaves that didn't get raked, blew away with the brisk fall winds that were soon ushering in the winter weather. The holidays were coming, the first being Thanksgiving Day.

Thanksgiving Day arrived and so did the scrumptious delicacies of the holiday. Ralph and his dad invited Grandma and Grandpa over for the feast. First and foremost the meal consisted of a giant turkey—almost twenty pounds. Mr. Eltison loved to eat leftovers, including two extra days of cold turkey sandwiches. A ham was also prepared, for no other reason other than his dad's love for ham sandwiches. Stuffing, mashed potatoes, cranberry sauce, and assorted vegetables were on the Thanksgiving Day menu. Biscuits, gravy, casseroles, sweet potatoes (for the adults, because not too many kids went for the sweet potatoes), and a mix of nuts and crackers were also added to the main course. Then there were the desserts. Apple, pumpkin, and cherry pies, along with puddings, a cake, and ice cream.

Now Elt was not even allowed at or around the table for normal dinner occasions. He would usually sit or lie just outside the kitchen door in the dining room, or eat his dinner at his food bowl. Thanksgiving was a rare occasion when some house rules changed, especially the eating place. The only times Ralph and his dad would eat in the dining room were special ones, like holidays.

Elt was allowed to stay in the dining room with the family, since that was the main place he stayed when Ralph and his dad ate at the kitchen table. Elt was also allowed to lick up the "scraps" from Ralph's plate. He had the opportunity to taste delicious turkey, gravy, stuffing, corn, and potatoes. Never had Elt tasted such a delectable dish before. Not even twice a week canned food that he received would even match that, for these were flavors Elt had never tasted before. He was in heaven.

Ralph's dad made sure that Grandma and Grandpa took plenty of leftovers home. Dinner had taken place around four o'clock, dessert shortly thereafter, but by eight o'clock, the guys were hungry again, and one more time Elt received a special treat after Ralph couldn't eat one more bite.

Thanksgiving weekend passed swiftly. The kids were out of school. Ralph's dad took a few days off, and even joined Ralph and Jenny on a couple of the daily walks. The walks were pleasant, the weather cool and crisp, and Mr. Eltison could see happiness in Ralph that he hadn't seen in quite awhile. Elt was the perfect gift for Ralph.

The year's first snowfall arrived in early December, one of many that would blanket Spring Valley from late fall to early spring. The final tally was nearly seven inches. It was a powdery snow, so making a snowman was a challenge for the neighborhood kids.

Spring Valley was used to plentiful amounts of snow, but the closing of school would depend on how cold it was and how much snow stuck to the roads. On that particular day, the kids continued to listen to their local radio and watched TV broadcasts, and finally came the news they wanted to hear. "All Spring Valley schools are closed."

"No school!" exclaimed Ralph.

The season's first snow meant the first snow for Elt and Bernadette. What was this white stuff and why did it fall from the sky? When Elt first ventured outside and witnessed the new spectacle of snow, he ran straight into his doghouse. He then peeked out and sniffed at the falling snow for a minute or two. Realizing that there was no danger, Elt tip-toed through the snow. He created an outlay of puppy prints everywhere he walked. In less than five minutes, Elt began frolicking in the snow. He ran, slid, jumped, and even dove into the drifts.

On special days like that day, walks were replaced by playtime in their yards, walking through several inches of snow for some reason was nowhere near the fun as snowball fights, sledding, and erecting snowmen, even with snows that didn't favor credible snowman building. Ralph would either walk Elt over to Jenny's house, or vice-versa. The kids would play with their dogs in the snow. Bernadette would run next to her friend Elt and Jenny and Ralph would do the same. After a soothing hot chocolate inside and a few more minutes out in the snow, it was time for Ralph and Elt to head home.

Besides the first snowfall, December brought in the most precious of holidays . . . . Christmas. Ralph and his dad bought a tree every year at a tree lot on Pleasant Grove Road. They would trim the tree that night at home, usually about three weeks before Christmas. The night would end with a cup of hot cocoa and an admiration of a job well done.

Christmas was going to be special because Ralph and his dad welcomed a new member of the family, Elt. The pup didn't really understand all the excitement, but would run around the house emphatically knowing that Ralph too was excited about something.

Ralph's dad hung brightly colored lights outside the house and wreaths on the front windows. All of the homes on Springhaven Court were magically lit for the season. Mrs. Yao set out the traditional white candle lights in her windows, while Mrs. Reed strung colored lights up on her bushes and a tall spruce tree in her front yard. Mr. Dawkins boasted a giant inflatable Santa Claus that lit up his entire house and yard.

The town, especially downtown Spring Valley, was decorated for the season. Garland and lights sprinkled the trees and lamp posts along Main and First Streets. All of the stores: Drexel's, Brown's, Gletzky's, and White's, displayed eye-catching festive lights and decorations in their storefront windows. Even the Palace Theatre's marquee was outlined with twinkle lights and garland. Mr. Feldman from the hardware store celebrated Hanukkah, but still decorated his storefront windows with bright and festive holiday decorations.

Ralph and his dad loved to walk downtown and admire the brilliant spectacle of Christmas, and all of downtown's splendor and grandeur. The lights sparkled, music played, and to top it all, it snowed. It was a wonderful experience.

Ralph and his dad attended church downtown. There were a few churches in town, but Ralph and his dad belonged to a church on Maple Avenue, which branched off First Street. Maple Avenue was appropriately named for its string of maple trees that lined the avenue on both sides. On Christmas Eve, along with every Sunday, Ralph and his dad would attend service at their church. They usually attended the early service on Christmas Eve, so they could return home early to prepare for the big day.

All of the excitement of Christmas was just too much for Elt; the tree, the lights, and especially the presents. What were those things wrapped up under the tree? The presents under the tree before

Christmas Day belonged to Grandma and Grandpa, some family friends, and business associates of Ralph's dad. Ralph's, his dad's, and Elt's presents would arrive, of course, on Christmas Day.

The irresistible urge of finding out what was inside the wrapping was too much for Elt. One day in December, while Ralph's dad was out and Ralph was in school, Elt had the house to himself. He sniffed each package under the tree. He had to know what was in each of them. Maybe there was a treat. The smell wasn't there, but oh well, Elt went for it.

Elt ripped open each package; some fully, some just half-torn. Grandma's gifts, Grandpa's gifts, heck even the gift for the paper boy was not safe from the wrath of Elt. It didn't matter, when Elt was finished, the scene resembled Christmas morning, except there was no Ralph, no Mr. Eltison, just Elt. Christmas wrapping paper was strewn about the whole living room. Elt never realized at the time he had done something wrong. He thought it was pretty fun, that ripping of paper and stuff.

When Ralph's dad entered the house, he stopped dead in his tracks. His "to do" list had a new priority and his plans for the day were definitely postponed. Elt left quite a mess to clean.

"Bad boy Elt," commanded Mr. Eltison.

At first, Elt was elated to see one of his humans, but after that reaction from his human, Elt began to realize what he had done was wrong. Elt lowered his head and lowered his tail underneath himself against his belly. He slowly gazed up at Ralph's dad.

Amazingly, while Ralph's dad started sorting through the ripped-up packages, he looked up to find Elt with a sizable piece of wrapping paper in his mouth. Elt dropped the piece of paper in front of Mr. Eltison and then retrieved another piece. Elt was helping clean up his mess.

"Well I'll be," commented Ralph's dad.

After the clean up job, Mr. Eltison walked into the kitchen, reached into the lower kitchen cabinet and grabbed a treat for Elt. While the pup's behavior was not favorable earlier, Elt's actions had proven that he was sorry for what he had done and he did help tidy up the mess.

Elt waited patiently that day for Ralph and his dad to finish re-wrapping all the gifts before he could get his afternoon walk.

Luckily, none of the gifts were damaged and it didn't take long for Ralph and his dad to re-wrap all of the presents.

Christmas Eve around the Eltison house was very peaceful. After Ralph and his dad returned from the early church service, they sat in front of the tree, listened to some holiday music, and watched the fire in the fireplace.

It was the second Christmas without Mrs. Eltison, so there was still sadness in their hearts, but the addition of Elt to the family helped soothe the hurt and brought back some joyfulness to their hearts. Ralph and his dad could only chuckle when Elt would roll his favorite red ball around recklessly. The pooch would bounce into the couch before the ball rolled under it.

Shortly after, Ralph ventured upstairs to bed while his dad read a book on his favorite recliner. Elt followed the boy upstairs. Ralph had no idea what presents lay waiting for him in the morning. He really hadn't wished for anything for Christmas. His birthday gift, Elt, pretty much topped the list. There was probably a toy or game that he may have wanted, but Elt was such a big part of his life. Nothing, not even the newest game, could compare to his puppy.

Ralph awoke Christmas morning to find Elt licking his face as usual, as that was indeed a daily ritual. Ralph peered out his window. The weather lady on the TV had called for snow, but nothing had fallen yet. It was just cloudy and cold.

Ralph and Elt bolted downstairs and discovered an array of presents that weren't there the night before. The big day had arrived! Elt behaved. He just sniffed a couple of presents, but made no mistake of tearing into any packages. He had learned his lesson.

Soon Ralph's dad awoke to find his boy and Elt waiting patiently for him in the living room. Ralph opened a few gifts and allowed Elt to tear into a package of his own. Hiding inside the wrapping paper was a new squeeze toy, one that resembled a steak. Elt also received doggie treats, which soon became a morning snack. A new grooming brush and a shiny red collar were amongst more gifts for the pooch. A new collar was needed, for Elt's neck was growing, and the old one was tight. The last gift for Elt was a brand new chew-bone.

After breakfast, Ralph and Elt played with their new stuff. Ralph played with a new game for his computer while Elt chewed on his new bone. Later in the day, Ralph and his dad drove over to

Grandma's and Grandpa's house for Christmas dinner. They watched a Christmas movie before they left. The snow only fell as flurries that day, so Spring Valley was unfortunately spared a white Christmas.

The holidays were excellent for Ralph and Elt. The boy and his dog still met Jenny and Bernadette during their winter break. Ralph and Jenny shared their Christmas stories while Elt and Bernadette walked stride-for-stride with each other during their afternoon walks.

New Year's Day brought Spring Valley's worst snowstorm in history. Nearly four feet of snow hit the area, crippling the town for days. Now Spring Valley received its share of snow in the winter, and the town's road crews were used to working overnights clearing the roads. This storm, however, hit heavy on a holiday, when everyone was home. By the time the workers started clearing the roads, over a foot of snow had fallen on the ground and roads, and it just kept falling.

Although Elt enjoyed the earlier snowfall, he was intimidated by the layers of powdery snow. He had trouble exiting his doggie door, and Ralph struggled to open the back door just to let Elt outside. All walks for Elt and Bernadette were postponed until the roads were clear.

The kids in Spring Valley had a blast! Although the storm occurred during their school break, their vacation was extended because of the road closures. When they could leave the house, Ralph and Jenny, along with kids from area neighborhoods, erected a snow mansion, sledded down hills, and held some pretty awesome snowball fights.

Winter displayed a few more snow and ice storms, but all in all, things calmed down after that mammoth storm on New Year's Day. Feldman's Hardware Store still managed to sell out of their snow shovels and salt bags by the end of February, but only a couple more days were missed due to the weather. There were not many more days of school missed, so summer vacation wouldn't be interrupted. For a kid, that was important.

As the winter's cold made way for the freshness and warmth of spring, Elt was becoming quite a canine. Still technically a pup, Elt had grown to almost three feet in length. He weighed about fifty pounds, and was still growing.

Elt's new red collar really stood out brilliantly against his shiny black and brown coat. Elt was indeed a perfect specimen. He was a happy pup, he ate well, and loved his humans.

Ralph was amazed at some of the feats that Elt could accomplish. Elt had mastered the elementary tricks. Sitting, rolling over, shaking paws, and playing dead were easy for Elt. He could jump and catch his red ball in mid-air. Running from the backyard to the front took no time. Elt's presence was also a plus, especially when dealing with unruly confrontations.

One afternoon, while Jenny and Ralph were walking Elt and Bernadette after school, the kids took the extra long walk to the playground on Schoolhouse Road. They were expecting a quiet walk to the park, but what they received was a run-in with Sam Meyers.

The bully, along with two of his friends, was leaving the park, where they had been playing baseball. Instead of passing by the two kids, Sam stopped right in front of Elt, causing Ralph to pull on Elt's leash and make him stop.

"Hey, look who we have here boys," boasted Sam. "It's Ralph and his girlfriend."

Jenny winced, her eyes narrowed and she frowned sourly, trying to impose a mean demeanor. Jenny, like most of the kids at school, didn't particularly care for Sam Meyers. She was one of the few who wasn't intimidated by the boy.

Ralph gulped and stared over at Jenny, who was still giving Sam the evil eye and mouth routine.

"We're just walking our dogs," replied Ralph quietly.

"We're just walking our dogs," mimicked Sam sarcastically.

The boys behind Sam laughed at his remark.

"They look like stupid dogs," continued Sam as he smirked.

Now Bernadette the Cocker Spaniel was small, but she could still growl and scare the mightiest of intruders, bullies, or any other "low life" that would cause trouble. But a growl from a little thing like her didn't seem so scary. Elt on the other hand, was another story. Elt had some size on his side. Elt growled lowly, and kept his sights on Sam Meyers.

"You know fellas," remarked Sam as he glanced back to his friends. "We're gonna need some money for the snack machines. All of that hitting of baseballs has made me hungry. How much money do you two losers have?"

"Uh, I don't have any money Sam," answered Ralph.

"And even if we did, we surely wouldn't give it to you," challenged Jenny.

Ralph was getting more nervous by the minute. He knew that Sam was up to no good and he also knew that Jenny wasn't going to back down. Elt sensed his human was in trouble.

"Then maybe we'll just have to shake it out of them," Sam replied.

Sam grabbed Ralph by the collar and started to pick him up off the ground. Elt couldn't take it anymore. His low growl turned into a shrieking, angry bark. Elt lunged fiercely at Sam, causing the bully to let Ralph free and fall backwards. Bernadette, wanting to chime in and assist Elt, let out her own shrilled yelp. The two boys behind Sam backed away. Ralph sensed that Sam was no longer a threat. He eased up on Elt's leash and allowed his dog to draw closer to the bully. All it took was one more fierce bark.

"Nice doggie," uttered Sam. The boy picked himself off the ground, and along with his two friends, quickly ran away. Relieved that the whole situation was over, Ralph glanced at Jenny and smiled. She returned the smile. Ralph bent down and hugged Elt. His dog was his watchdog and protector.

"Good boy!" exclaimed Ralph. "You were awesome!"

Elt licked his human's face and wagged his tail.

Jenny wasted no time thanking her Bernadette. She stooped down and gave her spaniel a great big hug.

"Awesome job, too!" interjected Jenny. "You two scared stupid Sam Meyers. He'll never mess with us again!"

Ralph and Jenny had escaped a very harrowing experience, thanks to Elt and Bernadette. Sam Meyers would think twice before ever confronting Ralph and Jenny again with any mean intentions. Ralph had a perfect bodyguard, who didn't like anyone messing with his human.

Elt had saved the day. He had fought off the neighborhood bully and sent him running home. Little did anyone know that Elt, Bernadette, and the rest of Spring Valley would have to defeat another bully, in fact three of them. Trouble had moved into town, and they had names; Frake, Jake, and Bull. Life in Spring Valley was about to change, and it was not for the better.

CHAPTER 7

SPRING VALLEY NATIONAL BANK ROBBED! That was the shocking headline printed on the front of the Spring Valley Herald newspaper one early spring morning. Ralph's dad, along with every citizen in Spring Valley, read the front page in both disbelief and shock. The newspaper would sometimes print bad news that was happening worldwide, but something this horrible happening in Spring Valley? How could the town's biggest bank fall prey to robbers? Who would do such a thing?

In this town, everybody knew each other. If someone needed money, surely the bank would give them a loan. A friend or neighbor would help another friend or neighbor in a time of need. No one needed to just take the money from a bank. It was inconceivable!

The most troubling part of it all that this wasn't the first robbery that the paper had reported. It was the biggest, though. A grocery store, a gas station, and just folks off the street reported that they were forced to give up their money. It was never the same number of bad guys doing the job. Sometimes it was one, and other times two. But the bank job? Well that took three of them. Suddenly it seemed, there was a crime spree.

The paper couldn't be wrong. Why would it report that kind of news if it wasn't true? What were the police doing about these horrible problems? Was it safe to go anywhere in Spring Valley?

"Must be some kind of misunderstanding," commented Mr. Eltison to himself as he read the headlines that morning.

Ralph had left for school that morning in mid-April. The school year had less than two months remaining, but even the excitement over summer vacation was greatly subdued because of the worry due to the crime spree in Spring Valley.

Soon after the New Year's blizzard had blanketed Spring Valley, trouble also blew into town. Crum's three henchmen rode into town in an old black sedan. They parked the car in front of a vacant store on Main Street that displayed a FOR SALE OR LEASE sign in the window. Not many stores or houses were empty in Spring Valley. Crum and his men were fortunate that day. Mr. Jessup used to run an old tailor shop there. Most of the town's menfolk had their suits hemmed at Jessup's. Women brought dresses and other apparel to the store for alterations. "No job too small" was Mr. Jessup's motto.

After his sixty-sixth birthday, Mr. Jessup contemplated retirement. His two daughters had families of their own, and weren't interested in managing the tailor shop.

A new men's clothing store had opened in an uptown shopping center in Spring Valley, and they offered free tailoring with the purchase of their suits, jackets, and other items. Business was slower, and with no one to continue the family business, Mr. Jessup decided to close his business after Christmas.

Mr. Gletzky of Gletzky's Department Store owned the property that Mr. Jessup had rented to run the tailor shop. The structure was on the corner of Pleasant Grove Road and Main Street, right next to the department store. The sign on the window instructed any interested buyers or renters to stop by and speak with Mr. Gletzky at the department store.

"Can I help you gentlemen?" asked Mr. Gletzky.

"Yes please," replied Frake. "We are interested in your vacant building next door."

"Are you interested in renting, young man?" questioned Mr. Gletzky.

"No sir," replied Frake. "My boss wants to buy your property."

So that's how it started. Crum came down one cold January morning to Spring Valley for the first time. He and his cohorts drove straight to the Spring Valley National Bank, on the corner of Main and First Streets, and met Mrs. Simon, the bank manager. They closed the deal on the old Jessup building, and Crum's men were delighted to purchase it and move in. It was all they needed to set up shop for their devious plan. As soon as the deal was completed, Crum quickly departed Spring Valley to attend to his evil doings in Bordertown.

"The air smells too clean here," grunted Crum, who was used to the smoke-filled air that Bordertown's factories produced.

While Frake, Bull, and Jake were residing in Spring Valley, Crum, Sid, and Jeb were running things in Bordertown. Sometimes Frake would leave Bull and Jake for a day to travel to and from Bordertown.

W.E.C. INSURANCE was the name imprinted on the front window of the new property on Main Street. A COMING SOON sign was hung above the front door. W.E.C., of course, were the initials of one Walter Eugene Crum. The business would never really open, it was just a ploy to show that a business was opening soon, so that all the citizens would think there was a new business replacing Jessup's.

The building on Main Street was their new hideout. It was three stories tall, but Crum's men only needed one floor to operate, so they immediately rented the two top floors to folks who just moved or needed a place to live. They charged them very high rent, just like they did to people living in Bordertown. The men set up beds and more furniture on the first floor. There was also a small kitchen and place to eat and watch television. They constructed a small lobby for the so-called insurance business, with a partitioned wall to hide their living quarters.

The area where the men ate their meals also served as a meeting room, just off the kitchen, where Frake and his boys would plan their next evil scheme. Against the wall in that room was a large gray safe, where they kept much of the goods that were stolen from the businesses and citizens of Spring Valley.

Shortly after they moved into their hideout, Frake and his boys began their diabolical mission to take over Spring Valley. They would start out small; robbing small businesses like a gas station. All the while, Frake made sure that the guys were seen as good citizens throughout the area, so they wouldn't arouse suspicion amongst the community. One day they would shovel snow off the sidewalks, and another day help an elderly lady across Main Street. Good deeds were always a sign of friendliness and good will.

Most of the robberies occurred at night, when it was hard to see who the robber was. Frake took the first job, and it worked. A man was pumping his gas at the Pump and Serve on Franklin Street. Franklin Street was a few miles away from downtown, in the direction of the suburban neighborhoods like Ralph's. When the man finished pumping his gas, Frake, dressed in all black and wearing a mask, demanded the money. The man had very little money, but Frake stole all that he had.

The incident wasn't reported until a couple of days later, when the man paid a visit to Sheriff Thomas at the Spring Valley Police Department, which was situated at the corner of First and Main Streets. The sheriff didn't really believe him. "A robbery? Here in Spring Valley?" He told the man that he would "look into it."

Next were some isolated reports of citizens being scared off by a "scary individual" at the Spring Valley Park on Pleasant Grove Road. The suspect was dressed in all black, wore a mask, and jumped out of the bushes or from behind a tree yelling "boo!" That scary person was Bull, and sometimes Jake. Kids who were scared off informed their parents, but no one was ever found, so parents figured it was just a practical joke by one of their kid's friends. Adults who were scared figured it was someone pulling a prank.

The crimes became more serious one late winter afternoon. The customers at the Eats-A-Lot Grocery Store in the Spring Valley Shopping Center were greeted with "This is a robbery!" by two men donned in black and wearing masks. The two men demanded money and jewelry from the customers and staff. The men grabbed cash from the register, and even loaded a grocery cart full of food on their way out.

One of the two men, Jake, calmly said, "This is the best service I've ever had. Thank you," before he and his cohort, Bull, left the store.

The robbery definitely made the front headlines of the Herald newspaper. Citizens who read the front page article couldn't believe it. Eyewitness accounts from both the customers and employees confirmed the robbery, so the story had to be true.

The Spring Valley Police Department, which was basically comprised of Sheriff Thomas and Deputy Taylor, was befuddled. All of these crimes and strange occurrences didn't fit a pattern. There weren't the same number of suspects at every crime. The events happened in different parts of town. The sheriff hadn't ever dealt with a situation like that before. Both men were scratching their heads. Who would do such a thing?

There were burglaries, too. Many downtown businesses, including Gletzky's and Feldman's, opened mornings to find either money or merchandise missing from their stores. Not a trace of entry or exit, just a bunch of money and "stuff" missing, according to the business owners.

"Must be outsiders," declared Sheriff Thomas. "Somebody who doesn't live here. It's got to be someone who just comes into town to rob our stores and citizens."

Well, the sheriff was half-way right, these bad guys did originate from Bordertown, but they also resided in town. In fact, they lived only minutes from the Spring Valley Police Station.

The biggest score for these guys was of course, the Spring Valley National Bank, for that's where all of Spring Valley's money was. Frake's plan was simple; rob the bank and we topple the town. Folks who lived in Spring Valley deposited their money there. When the residents of Spring Valley needed a loan for their home or business, the bank was where they went.

It was an ordinary early spring morning when Mrs. Samuels, the bank manager, opened the Spring Valley National Bank. She opened the doors for her employees, and at nine o'clock the staff opened their doors, inviting the customers who were waiting to enter.

Business was brisk in the morning, but started to slow down around ten-thirty. Frake and his boys knew exactly when to strike, when they arrived, only one customer was in line and the security guard had just stepped out for a cup of coffee.

In just a few minutes, the three of them, garbed in cartoon character masks and all black garments, escaped with numerous bags of cash. They ran out the back door and fled through the alley. They jumped into a white car, which they stole the night before from a used car lot uptown, and sped off. The men ditched the white car later that day on a road leading to Bordertown, they leaped into their black sedan, which was parked waiting for them, and headed back to town like nothing ever happened. Later that evening, when everyone was asleep, Frake and his men unloaded the vehicle and stored all of the cash in the big gray safe.

Sheriff Thomas was cruising around town on duty while the bank job occurred. Deputy Taylor was sitting at his desk at the station. After the robbery, he was stunned when the alarm rang. There must have been some kind of mistake, a false alarm maybe.

Mrs. Samuels was in shock. She stared at her employees for a couple of minutes, made sure they were safe, and then gathered herself as she sounded the alarm. It had only been sounded during tests performed by security technicians. Nothing like that had ever happened there before.

The alarm was deafening. It sounded like three sets of church bells ringing, not with a melody, just a straight-on loud clamor of bells alerting whoever was listening that something dreadful just occurred at the Spring Valley National Bank.

Deputy Taylor heard the alarm easily, since the bank was right across the street from the police station. He didn't receive a memo that day that the bank was going to be testing its alarms, so he quickly sprang from his chair and ran out the front doors of the station. Once he was outside and witnessed the commotion in front of the bank, he knew that something was definitely wrong. He summoned Sheriff Thomas on his radio and ran across the street to find Mrs. Samuels at the front doors of the bank.

News spread fast around town about the bank robbery, especially with the assistance of the Herald's front page headlines. The town's citizens couldn't fathom it. Their perfect little town, which they thought was safe, was safe no more.

"First the grocery store, now the bank," said one citizen to another as he walked quickly to his car. "What's next, our homes?"

That was the general feeling around town. The usually crowded downtown streets had very few people walking around. Folks stayed home, afraid to venture out.

Mayor Helms reassured the folks in front of City Hall everyday during his morning greetings. He could see it in their faces. They were scared. Who was doing this to his town?

The mayor called an emergency meeting with Sheriff Thomas and some business leaders a few days after the bank robbery. Mr. Gletzky, Mrs. Samuels, Mr. Drexel, Mr. and Mrs. Brown, and Mr. Feldman were among the leaders in attendance.

"I don't know what to tell you," said a dejected Sheriff Thomas. "We have no leads. Sometimes it's one person, another time it's two, and the bank robbery had three suspects. We need more clues, eyewitness accounts, and even a license plate would help right now."

"We think our suspects may come from another town," interjected Mayor Helms.

"It's our best guess right now," said Sheriff Thomas. "But we're not sure."

"We have to stick together," said a determined Mrs. Brown. "We have to return Spring Valley back to the way it was."

"I hope we can," replied Sheriff Thomas. "Deputy Taylor and I are doing the best we can. We need help from our business leaders, citizens . . . . we really need everyone's assistance to catch these miscreants and restore our town back to the way it was."

The business leaders, the mayor, and the sheriff agreed to remain strong through the difficult period. But there was an underlying feeling of uneasiness in the room. None of these folks had ever dealt with a situation like this before. They really needed help.

Bad news about the town usually traveled through the words printed in the Herald every day, along with radio and television broadcasts. The bearer of the unfortunate news in the Eltison household was Elt, for every morning he was in charge of retrieving the newspaper from the front walk and delivering it to Ralph's dad. Elt would venture outside through his doggie door, down his back steps, and pick up the paper on the front sidewalk. He would deliver the paper by setting it down on Mr. Eltison's kitchen chair.

One morning, not too long after the bank robbery, Elt had retrieved the newspaper, and was heading to the backyard. Ralph was inside dressing for school and Ralph's dad was preparing breakfast for Ralph. Elt was turning the corner when he heard a strange voice behind him.

"Wow, must have been a long winter, you've really grown," said the female voice.

Elt's ears popped up. Perched on his fence was Jasmine, Mrs. Reed's tabby cat.

"You understand what I'm saying?" asked Jasmine. "I am fluent in both dog and cat speak."

Elt dropped the paper. He gazed at the strange animal. He had never seen an animal like that before, so he didn't know whether to be alarmed or not. Some instinct inside him said to be on alert.

"I understand," answered Elt. "But something inside of me is telling me to bark and chase you."

"You don't know what I am, do you?" asked Jasmine.

Elt shook his head no.

"Let's just say our sides have not always gotten along," replied Jasmine as she sprang from her perch and edged closer to Elt.

There was an eerie silence for a few seconds. Elt didn't know what to do next, so he just figured being friendly was the right thing to do.

"I'm Elt," said the dog to Jasmine.

"I know," said the tabby. "And I'm Jasmine."

"It's really nice to meet you," returned Elt, "but I have to get this paper to my human."

"Well, I'll be quick Elt," said Jasmine. "I want to let you know that you've been invited to our first neighborhood canine-feline meeting of the year."

"Meeting?" asked Elt.

"Oh yes," Jasmine answered. "The dogs around our neighborhood and me, of course being the only cat in the immediate area, meet every full moon, except for when the snow comes. We usually meet at one dog's tool shed, but if you and your friend come, we will need to find a bigger meeting place."

"Friend?" asked Elt.

"Why Bernadette my dear boy," answered Jasmine. "You walk with her every day. Surely she can come with you to the meeting."

Elt couldn't figure how this strange little animal knew so much about him and Bernadette, and never noticed that a cat had been spying on him.

"I'll see her today, and let her know about the meeting," stated Elt.

"Then we'll see you tomorrow at Juan's garage," said Jasmine.

"Juan's garage?" asked Elt.

"You know, that over-excited Chihuahua that lives on the corner house up ahead," stated Jasmine.

Elt thought for a few seconds, and then remembered a little dog scurrying around a house on the corner of Valleydale and Schoolhouse Roads.

"Okay, when should I . . . . I mean we . . . . be there tomorrow?" asked Elt.

"When the sun is straight up in the sky," remarked Jasmine. "See you tomorrow!"

Jasmine ran across Elt's yard, leaped to the fence, and then landed into Mr. Dawkins's front yard. She pounced in front of Prince the Doberman, who had just rounded the corner of his house. Jasmine could tell that her little tease, running in front of Prince, bothered him. But she also knew that he would ignore her. She could easily outrun him, so she didn't make a move or he would have been embarrassed.

"No time to be playing your silly little game," announced Prince to Jasmine. "I'm on watch this morning, looking for those bad humans my human has been talking about."

"Interesting," remarked Jasmine.

She then jumped back on the fence, ran through Elt's yard past the pup, who had been watching the whole scene, and then leaped to the safety of her own yard.

The upcoming trip out of the yard was going to be a big test for Elt. Elt had never been outside the yard without his human, and that meant he hadn't been alone outside his own yard since the day Mr. Drexel found him in the alley behind the pet store. He would have to be brave, being without a leash meant he was on his own. Elt would have to be aware of cars, other animals, and especially . . . . humans. He would have to stay out of sight. He wouldn't want Mr. Eltison to catch sight of him trying to escape.

Later that day on their walk, Elt proposed the idea of attending the neighborhood pet meeting with Bernadette. She was a little apprehensive about leaving her yard, but thought that a meeting was a great idea to meet all the neighborhood pets. While Ralph and Jenny stopped for a break, the two pooches had a chance to communicate.

Elt and Bernadette had to create a plan and do it fast, as they were taking a short walk and the meeting was the next day. If they failed to reach Juan's garage the next day, they may never get invited again. Before they departed, Elt made sure that Bernadette was ready. She gave him the nod as she walked off with Jenny.

The next day brought sunshine and warmer temperatures to Spring Valley. A family of robins had moved into the Eltison backyard willow tree. Their chirps brought a peaceful atmosphere to Ralph's backyard. It was close to noon. The sun was close to its midpoint.

Ralph's dad had left the house to run a few errands and deliver some paperwork to a couple of clients. He stepped into his truck and drove away. Elt knew that it was the perfect time to depart. He exited the kitchen through his doggie door and proceeded to the front of the yard.

Elt stopped at the front gate. Luckily, the gate wasn't latched tightly, so Elt easily nudged the latch open. Making sure he wasn't noticed, Elt eased through the gate opening he created and then raced over to Bernadette's house.

Mrs. Rodgers was at work for most of the day, so the Cocker Spaniel had plenty of time to leave and return. Elt on the other hand, had less time. He knew that Ralph's dad was never gone too long before returning. Bernadette had barked at the door that morning before Mrs. Rodgers left, so Jenny's mom let her out for the day until she returned.

Elt ran all the way to Bernadette's house. She was waiting for him at the front gate. Being the taller of the two dogs, it was easier for Elt to manipulate the gate latch. Before too long, their persistence paid off. The gate latch opened. The two dogs slipped out of the opening, checked for cars and humans, and then sped over to the house on the corner of Valleydale and Schoolhouse Roads.

Jasmine, perched on the front fence in Juan's yard, awaited the dogs's arrival, and directed them to the back part of the house towards the garage.

"You're just in time," stated Jasmine as she caught up with Elt and Bernadette.

Bernadette had seen Jasmine before, unlike Elt, but still didn't know what to think of the strange looking animal.

The dogs entered the garage through a side door that was hardly ever used by Mrs. Perez. Once inside, Juan was there to greet them.

Juan laid a small piece of carpet for all the dogs to sit on during the meeting.

"Mi casa es su casa," greeted Juan to every dog and cat that entered. He also set out a bowl of doggie treats next to the entrance.

Sarge and Chin were already inside by the time Elt and Bernadette had reached Juan's front yard. Old Max hadn't shown up yet.

"Place is kind of big . . . . too fancy for me," blurted Sarge when he first entered the garage. He grabbed a couple of biscuits and started eating them.

The garage was immaculately clean. Mrs. Perez kept it spotless. It was extremely spacious on that day because her car was gone while she was out shopping. There were even rafters above for Jasmine to climb on.

Sarge's last biscuit never made it to his mouth, for he noticed Elt and Bernadette making their way towards him and Chin.

"I don't believe it," said Sarge. "Those little stinkers showed up."

"They aren't little anymore," Jasmine stated, peering down below at Sarge from the rafters. "Elt is going to be quite a dog. He's not fully grown yet either."

"Well, as long as I'm in the neighborhood, I'll still be the boss!" blasted Sarge.

For Elt and Bernadette, the first experience of being out on their own was not only exciting, it was astonishing. They were in a new place . . . . a really nice, new place. Plus they were going to meet all the pets from the neighborhood.

"This is awesome!" exalted Bernadette.

In awe of the whole event, Elt and Bernadette walked slowly towards the Boxer. Sarge defiantly stood his ground. Out of respect, and to the shock of the Boxer, Elt and Bernadette both bowed their heads to acknowledge the elder Sarge. He proudly accepted the gesture with a nod of his own.

"It's an honor to meet you," declared Elt.

Sarge was not only surprised, but he was a little humbled, he didn't expect such courtesy from a younger pup. Jasmine snickered from above. All Sarge could do was utter a simple "Hello, nice to meet you both."

"They should be bowing to the oldest guy here you know," announced Max jokingly as he entered the room. "I'm the oldest one here."

Max walked over slowly to Sarge, Elt, and Bernadette.

"You must be Elt and Bernadette . . . . welcome to the neighborhood," said the Sheepdog. "You'll love it here in our neighborhood. We have excellent humans."

"Pleasure to meet you all," replied Bernadette as she gazed at everyone in the room.

"Have you welcomed our new neighbors, Chin?" asked Max.

Chin just grinned and continued to chew on a tasty bone.

"Okay, enough talk," Sarge blurted. "Let's get this meeting started! This is our first official meeting since before the last snowfall."

Sarge stepped in front of everyone. Juan nudged the side door shut. The dogs all sat down and formed a small row in front of the Boxer. Jasmine jumped down to a work table that was next to everyone else.

"Now to the business at hand," continued Sarge. "I think we all know what we're going to talk about today. I hear the barks from other dogs all around town."

Chin, Juan, Max, and Jasmine all agreed. Elt and Bernadette, however, didn't have a clue. They were of course young pups, both under a year old. During their times together on the walks or playtime in their yards, they never really cared about the warning barks and howls in the far off distance. But now they sensed a silence, a worry that was felt throughout the room.

"My human said it was the worst thing to hit Spring Valley ever," Sarge declared.

"What is going on here?" asked Elt. "What are we all supposed to be worried about?"

The room fell silent.

"Bad humans!" shouted Max. "Some of these bad humans are doing terrible things in our town! Our humans are scared! They want to leave town if things don't get better. Our town is in big trouble!"

"What can we do?" questioned Bernadette.

"Protect our houses and neighborhood!" roared Sarge.

"Talk to each other, make sure our humans are safe!" added Juan.

Bernadette and Elt watched the older dogs intensely. They listened to every word they barked. They learned quite a bit in a very short time.

"Keep an eye out for suspicious characters," added Max. "Warn us all, and we can pass it through to our dogs in the next neighborhood."

"Be alert at all times!" exclaimed Sarge.

The message was clear. The meeting was about nothing else. Not only were the humans of Spring Valley concerned about the recent changes in their town, the uneasy feelings had trickled down to their pets. Something had to be done to stop the bad news.

It was time for the meeting to adjourn. It was time for the dogs and cat to leave before Mrs. Perez came home. Although Elt and Bernadette were unaware of how the dogs ended their meetings, they waited for Sarge to make the announcement. Sarge, Max, Juan, and Jasmine turned their attention to the Chow Chow. Elt and Bernadette followed suit by turning their heads to watch Chin. The Chow Chow took a deep breath.

"Sugar and spice make good cookies," announced a smiling Chin.

"That's sugar and spice makes everything nice, you knucklehead!" exclaimed Sarge. He shook his head in disbelief.

The other dogs, including Elt and Bernadette, along with Jasmine, thought long and hard about Chin's words of wisdom, but could make nothing of it.

"Meeting adjourned!" declared Sarge. "We'll meet next full moon unless we call an emergency meeting."

The dogs slowly filed away from Mrs. Perez's garage. Sarge stuffed about three biscuits in his mouth before he left. Elt and Bernadette walked back to their houses, not as concerned as before about being seen. Their little world had been rocked. Everything had been great. Going on walks, playing with their humans, and having a warm comfy house to sleep in were parts of their wonderful world. Now a new world had opened up to them, and it wasn't warm and comfy.

Their neighborhood; their safe houses to play, were not safe. Although technically nothing had really happened in the Valleydale subdivision, according to the leaders of the neighborhood pets, the whole area was under alert. Elt and Bernadette hardly even said "bye" to each other before Elt left. Elt made it to his yard, slipped through the doggie door, and simply laid down in the living room, awaiting either Ralph's or Mr. Eltison's return.

News from the dog hideout was dismal. Never had a meeting been so down, yet so meaningful. Changes had to be made.

Now news at another hideout was not so dismal. On that evening, a few days after the bank robbery, a special meeting was held at the W.E.C. Insurance building. Walter E. Crum was in attendance. He brought with him his two other men, Sid and Jeb.

The visit's purpose was to see how things were going . . . . how well Crum's and Frake's plan was working. They sat at the table eating dinner, which was a very unpleasant experience for Crum.

"Why do I do this to myself?" grumbled Crum to himself. "It's a despicable sight . . . just horrific!"

What Crum was referring to was whenever he and his men called a meeting around lunch or dinner time, Crum had to watch these five overgrown monsters eat, which itself was a very bad lesson in table manners. Although Frake and his men carried themselves professionally in their jobs, deep down they were ruthless brutes. The sight of these five "animals" gorging themselves was a disgusting sight for anyone to witness, yet alone an old bitter man like Crum.

The dinner consisted of chickens, roasts, potatoes, biscuits, vegetables, and desserts. Before the meal commenced, the table was filled to the brim with food and drinks. The aftermath, however, showed that there was very little food left . . . . just scraps and bones. There were food fragments strewn all over the floor below, too.

Frake's unshaven face was covered with mashed potatoes. Sid, well you couldn't tell it was Sid by all the food on his face. Jake and Bull . . . . their napkins stayed clean, because they didn't use them. Jeb never shut his mouth while he ate.

The sight Crum did love was the opened safe that was filled with cash and valuables. He requested it stay open during the dinner.

"All right, let's get on with this," demanded Crum. "I'd like to get back to Bordertown tonight."

"Well Mr. Crum," replied Frake, "as you can see, things are going according to plan. We've scared the people of this town, and we're using their money that we stole to buy up as many properties as we can."

"How many people are leaving?" asked Crum.

"Three houses are up for sale this month," answered Frake. "We should close on all of them by the end of the month. Next month we expect to buy five more."

"Excellent! Excellent!" exclaimed Crum. "Lay low for awhile, then strike them back at the bank again when their guard is down. We'll take more of their money!"

"Boss, do you want us to take any of the money that's in the safe back to Bordertown with us?" asked Sid.

"No, we have plenty of money back home," replied their ruthless leader. The old man's eyes gleamed at the sight of all that cash and valuables in the safe. "Stay on course gentlemen, and soon this town will be ours!"

Crum, Jeb, and Sid returned to Bordertown that night, leaving the other men in Spring Valley to carry on with their master plan of turning Spring Valley into another Bordertown. The plan was working. People in Spring Valley were scared. They were selling their houses and leaving. Crum's men would buy the houses for a cheap price and then rent them out for higher prices to unsuspecting newcomers who had originally heard that Spring Valley was a wonderful place to live. With more and more houses and soon more businesses under Crum's control, lives in Spring Valley and Bordertown would be no different.

Elt thought long and hard that night about what he had to do. On his last trip outside to do his business before going to bed with Ralph, Elt listened to the barks from far away for the first time. This was all new to him. He was amazed at the sounds he heard from so far off, many neighborhoods away from his own.

"All quiet tonight," Elt whispered to himself.

Elt felt a sense of duty to be on guard. Now he knew that his purpose in life was not only to be a playtime partner with Ralph, but he had to be a protector of his humans and his home. He had saved Ralph earlier from the clutches of a bully. Now he had to save his humans and his neighborhood from some unknown bullies who were scaring the humans into leaving their beloved town.

Who were these unknown bullies and where did they come from? Why did they come? And how were the dogs and cats of this town going to protect their neighborhoods and their town?

Elt's duties as Ralph's pet were now set in his mind. He had to carry on with the daily walks with Ralph, Jenny, and Bernadette. He would still play games with Ralph, eat with his humans, and continue to fetch the newspaper for Ralph's dad. He would still lay quietly in the living room while Ralph read or worked on his homework. But he would always have to be on guard and ready to protect his home if the need arrived.

Although it was just another day in his short life, for Elt it was different. The neighborhood pet meeting had changed his whole way of thinking. Elt was not even a year old, but he would have to grow up fast.

Little did Elt and the rest of Spring Valley know that help was on its way. Not from the police department. Not from the army. Not from any human or animal at all. In fact, help was coming, not from this world, but one from very far away.

CHAPTER 8

WE'RE COMING UP ON OUR destination now," said the first officer.

"Carry on," said the captain.

"Sir, may I once again kindly object to the wearing of our distransulators before we initiate contact," returned the first officer.

"Like I've told you before on many occasions, I like to use the language we will be speaking for awhile," said the captain. "Just in case we engage in an unfortunate encounter with one of their beings. We will be landing on a quadrant of this planet that has a difficult language to understand. They call it English."

"I understand sir," returned the first officer. "These devices are just so uncomfortable."

"One would think that with our advanced technologies we could discover a less intrusive version of this language decoder," replied the captain. "No other device our scientists have constructed work as well as this bulky one that hangs around our bodies. It decodes millions of different languages. We wouldn't be able to do what we do without them."

There was a strange glow that illuminated the unusually dark spaceship bridge. A greenish glowing light didn't originate from the ship itself. It came from the inhabitants.

Now numerous reports and stories involving aliens from far away worlds involve the conquering of Earth or the takeover of the human race. These aliens were desperate, mean-spirited beings that thought nothing more than to dominate the planet and make it their own. There were aliens like that, if it ever could be proven, but there were some who liked to help instead of destroy. These adventurous voyagers traveled from solar system to solar system, planet to planet, helping civilizations in need.

This particular species of aliens were called Trianthians. They originated from a planet called Trianthius. Their captain on the ship, who was also one of their elder leaders, was named Coladeus. Coladeus and his group traveled for many duraceps (a duracep was equal to about two Earth years), aiding troubled situations on various planets. Whether it was aiding in relief on a poor planet, helping to re-vegetate a dying planet, or just re-energizing an out-manned race that was being dominated by an evil aggressor, the Trianthians had one purpose; for good to triumph over evil.

Coladeus and his band of warriors had to be careful. They just couldn't land somewhere and stick themselves in the middle of a situation. They had to stay inconspicuous, so they had to choose their "missions" carefully. Some jobs were just too big for them, such as civil wars that lasted for many years. Coladeus had to choose assignments that he felt were best suited for their purpose. He would also have to find a medium in which to transfer his assistance through. His race was advanced technically, but transforming their bodies to resemble the races of beings they were assisting was not possible. The Trianthians possessed the distransulators, which helped them communicate with their mediums. They did possess some powers, but again, they were traveling to help, not destroy.

The planet Trianthius was named for its triangular shape. Most planets were shaped like circles or spheres. Trianthius resembled a giant pyramid, a glowing green one in fact. Gaseous on its surface, but full of vegetation and life, their planet rotated around its sun, but their sun was very far away, so daily sunlight was almost non-existent. In fact, the planet stayed pretty dark all of the time. But then there was that strange green glow that not only came from the Trianthians, but from the planet itself.

Much like the depths of Earth's seas, where there is no light at all, life existed heartily on this planet. Trianthians possessed a rare gift that allowed them to see and be seen. Both the deep sea creatures of Earth and the Trianthians glowed in the dark, a strange greenish-yellowish glow to be exact. What made Trianthians so special was that they could turn on their glow when they wanted through mind control.

The planet was comprised of phosphorus-like rock that the Trianthians fed off constantly. So basically the energy from the planet made them glow. When they rested, they could conserve their energy and turn off their glow for awhile.

Now when Trianthians like Coladeus and his crew traveled, which was basically most of the time, they needed the energy from their planet to live, so they had to invent a way to transfer the energy from their planet to their ship. To the Trianthians, the phosphorus-like rock was the equivalent of oxygen to humans; they devised a machine that would transmit the energy from the rocks they brought on board to energize each Trianthian. So before they left for one of their journeys, Coladeus and his crew made sure that they carried a plentiful supply of Trianthian crystals on their spaceship before they departed.

Coladeus was a veteran of many successful trips around countless solar systems throughout the universe. He had traveled to Earth before, many duraceps ago, so he was familiar with the planet somewhat. He and his crew brought food and medical relief into big cities during times of crisis. They had used animals, especially dogs, as mediums to help them deliver food to many needy families.

The Trianthian crew of eight traveled in a rather modest spaceship, about the size of two modern day train cars. The spaceship was shaped like a triangle, kind of like a miniature model of their planet. The ship was deep, for it contained three levels. The top floor consisted of the control room or bridge, and Coladeus's small living quarters. The second level consisted of the crew's living quarters, which was one big room, and most important of all, the regeneration chamber, where the Trianthians re-energized their glow. The lower level consisted of the engine room, and a space for their small pod ship, which was shaped like an egg.

Coladeus preferred using the pod ship for travel from his ship to his destination during his missions. The pod, of course, was such smaller and easier to hide when landing on a planet. The pod could seat two passengers.

The spaceship and the pod were fueled by the same energy that sustained the Trianthian's lives; the Trianthian crystals. Each piece of crystal, which was about the size of a human hand, could continue to supply energy to each member of the crew for about half a duracep. Larger pieces easily fed the ship and pod. The pod mainly was released into a planet's atmosphere and usually didn't need any fuel, only enough to get it back off the ground and toward the ship.

The ship was named Trianthius I, the first of three ships built to carry on their goodwill missions. Sometimes all three ships were deployed at the same time, with two other elder leaders voyaging to other outreaches in space. Most of the time, two were deployed, so that one ship could be docked and ready for emergency situations.

Coladeus was the only original member of Trianthius I. A shipmate's duty wasn't life long, for after ten duraceps, members could transfer to different ships, remain and work on the home planet, or just retire.

Trianthius I was on a peaceful mission, but still had to be fortified. Firing missile-style rays of light, or "litoses" as they were called, had only been carried out once or twice in their ship's history. Once again these rays were powered by Trianthian crystals, but to a very high degree. A litoses ray could melt anything it touched.

Trianthians were very small compared to humans; the average height of a Trianthian was about four feet tall when it was mature. Eating was not a concern for these aliens, for a short time in the re-generating chamber made them healthier than ever. Re-energizing in the chamber usually took only a few minutes and transpired weekly. The crystals that lasted up to half a duracep could be used weekly. On the planet, of course, Trianthians were re-energized just from being surrounded by all of the existing rock on their planet. Although they didn't eat daily, it was said that Trianthians nibbled on various types of vegetation on their planet and enjoyed the nectar out of certain plants, especially honeysuckle flowers on planet Earth.

Although Trianthius was comprised mostly of rock, the planet was blessed with many rain forest-like areas. The climate usually remained the same; mild and warm. Rains arrived twice a duracep, and lasted about two Earth weeks.

Coladeus would return to his planet about once a duracep. He would meet with his council of elders, relax and spend time with his family, and gather supplies for his next voyage. He also spent time organizing crew training before the crew would venture out again.

"Let's review the file on our next destination again Matheun," commanded Coladeus to his first officer.

Matheun, a veteran himself of numerous voyages and missions, would soon command his own ship, either when Coladeus retired or if the Trianthian elders decided to expand its fleet of ships in the future. The first officer had traveled with his captain for the last three duraceps, and was well-trained in handling any adverse situation; from steering through a meteor shower to responding to an enemy attack. Matheun peered through a scope-like screen for a few seconds.

"It's the fourth planet in the Zectar system sir," replied Matheun.

"That planet would be called Earth," stated Coladeus.

"That is affirmative," answered a surprised Matheun. "But how did you . . . . ?"

Coladeus rose from his seat. "It's not the first time we've been here," declared the captain. "This planet has a troubled past. Long before you joined our crew, we visited this planet and helped restore peace in many unsettled areas. Now it needs our help again. The mission is simple, but if we don't correct the situation, things will only get worse."

Coladeus's words were true. It was not known when Coladeus had visited and helped restore order to Earth, but the planet's history was still fresh in the leader's mind. Whether it was one of the world wars, or the Great Depression, the outcome of Earth's history could have been decided by the efforts of the Trianthians.

Coladeus, like all Trianthians, possessed special powers that were generated by the crystals. The powers were used for positive purposes only, and he always delivered his powers through a medium, either to a being or animal from that planet. Coladeus and other elder members possessed far greater powers than the typical Trianthian.

The living beings that Coladeus would transfer his powers to varied from planet to planet. Each planet hosted different living beings. For instance, on their last mission, Coladeus transferred powers to several children on the planet to face numerous misbehaving and unlawful adults.

What kind of super powers? Depending on how much glowing crystal was given to the receiver, powers could consist of super strength, extreme speed, incredible leaping, and in some cases, flying. Now if a human was given these powers, he or she would have to be trusted not to use them for his or her personal gain. The main reason Coladeus didn't want to transfer powers to a human is that in order to transfer the powers to a human, a human and a Trianthian would have to make contact. That wasn't a good idea at all.

On Earth, avoiding contact with humans was a must. Coladeus was well aware of the human race's fascination with beings from outer space. Although he was quite confident he could escape any situation that involved Trianthians and humans, Coladeus knew that avoidance with human contact was his utmost concern.

Matheun scanned his computer screen.

"Coladeus, I'm reading our history of our travels to Earth," stated Matheun. "Are we are going to the same quadrant as before?"

"Yes, disturbances have stirred up once again in that region," replied Coladeus.

Matheun continued to study his scanner.

"Coladeus, it seems we have discovered a new danger in a quadrant we've never visited before," stated Matheun.

Puzzled, Coladeus rose and drifted over to Matheun's scanner.

"Let me take a look," he replied. "Interesting."

Coladeus paused for a moment.

"Seems like crimes and acts of unkindness have risen six hundred percent," reported Matheun as he continued to read from his scanner. "A place that had virtually no crime now has events that have never happened there before."

"Let's take a closer look," said Coladeus.

Matheun pushed a few buttons on his console. A screenless image, resembling something like a movie, popped up in front of them. An external map of Earth closed in on North America, then closed in on mid-America, then to a mountain range, and then stopping at a satellite image of Spring Valley and Bordertown.

How did the Trianthians scope out planets so quickly? An advanced satellite system, a very sophisticated one, was a valuable tool used on board Trianthius I that Coladeus and his crew needed in order to execute their missions. The system could scan a planet's interior, exterior, and even the depths of the oceans.

"Here is the area," commented Matheun. "The town is named Spring Valley. Human population, approximately fifteen thousand."

The picture zoomed in on the town. It focused on Main Street, with citizens rushing by on a busy afternoon. Coladeus noticed the uneasiness of the humans's actions, sensing fear in them.

"All is quiet, but not quite right," mentioned Coladeus. "Do we have more information?"

"Yes," replied Matheun.

With a few clicks of switches on his console, Matheun switched the picture in front of them to a scene in downtown Bordertown. Its dirty streets were lined with somber folks with very long faces. The smoke of the nearby factories billowed out behind the decayed downtown buildings.

"This is the closest town to Spring Valley," reported Matheun. "It is called Bordertown."

Coladeus studied the picture in front of him carefully.

"What we are witnessing here may be the cause of our situation in Spring Valley," stated the Trianthian leader. "Who on Earth are we using as mediums?"

Matheun continued to view his scanner.

"The canine, said Matheun. "It is quick, smart, and possesses both the natural abilities and anatomies that are sufficient enough to receive our powers."

"Have we found our prospect yet?" asked Coladeus.

"I'm already ahead of you," replied Matheun.

Matheun switched to an image of the Valleydale subdivison of Spring Valley. The picture zoomed in on Ralph and Jenny walking their dogs on Valleydale Drive. Matheun zoomed further in on Bernadette first, and then stopped at Elt.

"Here is our prospect," stated Matheun. "He is still growing, but is strong, healthy and intelligent. He's teachable, because he's still young, not quite one Earth year old according to our readings."

The Trianthians watched Ralph and Elt enter their yard.

"Yes, the older ones can be a little difficult to work with," responded Coladeus. "The prospect looks excellent."

“So we should alter our course?” asked Matheun.

“Yes, definitely change course to this Spring Valley,” replied Coladeus. “We will go to Spring Valley first, and then we will stop by our original destination.”

With a click of a few switches, Trianthius I changed course and maneuvered its way to Earth, closing in on Spring Valley, and even further right into the Valleydale subdivision.

On that very day in May, Ralph and Jenny had walked their dogs after school, not realizing that they were being watched by beings from a world far away.

Sweaters, jeans, and coats made way for short sleeves and short pants, for spring was giving way to summer. Elt sported his new collar, his third one, he had already outgrown the collar he received at Christmas. Ralph picked a new color for Elt. Oddly enough it was neon green, and the collar really stood out against Elt’s brown and black hair. The new collar had caught Ralph’s attention when he saw it on display at Drexel’s Pet Store. He knew Elt would need a new collar soon, so he pleaded with his dad. Ralph’s dad advanced Ralph’s allowance a couple of weeks so the boy could purchase the collar.

All the neighborhood dogs plus Jasmine caught a glimpse of Elt’s new collar. They were all impressed, except for Prince. The Doberman wasn’t impressed when he noticed Elt while walking in his yard.

“Oh, isn’t he Mr. Fancy?” questioned Prince.

Prince wore the most expensive collar sold at Drexel’s. It was light brown in color with diamond-shaped studs all around it. In Mr. Dawkin’s mind, Prince was the most impressive creature on Earth. Only the finest collar would do for Prince.

On that night, a Friday night, Ralph and his dad went out to their favorite restaurant, Brown’s. It was kind of like a ritual for them. One night when Mr. Eltison didn’t have to cook was a good reason to go out, too. Ralph loved their cheeseburgers, fries, and chocolate milk shakes. Mr. Eltison usually ordered a salad, but every once in awhile he would treat himself to a steak and baked potato.

Back on board the Trianthius I, Matheun broke away from his scanner and turned to speak to Coladeus.

“It’s time to board the pod,” said Matheun.

Coladeus rose and walked over to the bridge elevator. Once on the lower level, Coladeus approached the pod. The egg-shaped vessel's door was open. Multi-colored lights illuminated the otherwise dark interior. A Trianthian crew member handed Coladeus a small triangular-shaped container as the leader entered the pod. Once inside, Coladeus removed a small object from the box and inserted it inside a small pouch around Coladeus's abdomen.

Coladeus sat down on one of the two available seats. He pushed a series of buttons. The ship's door closed. The pod's engines started. Although it was a pod, it still was a spaceship, for it needed engines in order to get back to the mother ship. Sometimes the Trianthians had to readjust their course for a safe landing, so they would use the pod's engines to make those important adjustments.

Trianthius I's bay door opened. The pod, which rested on a sliding platform, began to move towards the opening. Coladeus waited patiently as the pod finished its run to the end of the platform. With one final push of a button from Coladeus, the pod's engines ignited, and the pod was thrusted into the Earth's atmosphere. Once he was well into the atmosphere, Coladeus cut his engines off and glided down towards the planet. He knew he had to save the pod's energy for the trip back to his ship.

The ship was so small it couldn't be detected by instruments on Earth. Coladeus locked onto the pod's navigational system. He entered the coordinates for Spring Valley into his computer. The pod zoomed at an incredible speed. Coladeus would have to slow down soon. Luckily, the pod was equipped to handle the task. With a pull of a lever from Coladeus, the small vessel started spinning around, making the ship decrease its speed by causing resistance.

It was very clear that evening, so clear, that Coladeus didn't have to battle any cloudiness to reach his destination. Stars as far as the eyes could see was the view for the Trianthian leader as he slowly spun his way to Spring Valley. The pod ship passed over the twinkling lights of downtown, the darkness of the park, and edged in to the Valleydale subdivision.

"This should be the one," Coladeus calmly told himself as he slowly landed his vessel in the Eltison backyard. Still spinning, the pod ship landed in the grass.

Elt had been lying on the living room floor next to the couch when he heard a strange noise coming from the backyard. With his ears perked and his tail straight up, Elt cautiously walked to the kitchen. He nudged open the doggie door and peeked out. In the darkness, Elt could barely see the egg-shaped ship. He sniffed the air for a clue. Nothing. Well, nothing he had ever sniffed before. Elt lowered himself and crawled slowly to the steps.

"Protect my human's house," Elt thought to himself as he slowly approached the strange object in his yard. He could make out its form, it stood much taller than it seemed from the porch.

Suddenly, to Elt's surprise, there was a hiss and the hatch door to the pod slowly opened. The steam emitted from the opening clouded Elt's vision. Then there was silence, except for a far off distant bark a few blocks away. Elt wasn't focused on those barks right now. There wasn't anything going on in all of Spring Valley that was more intense than what was occurring in his own backyard. There were no warnings about this. He had to protect his home. Elt reacted the only way he knew.

He belted out a series of yelps and barks. First, to warn whatever was inside that egg-shaped thing in front of him. Second, to warn others in his neighborhood about the strange intruder in his own backyard. Could this have been part of what was troubling the humans?

After a few more series of barks, Elt stopped, it was at that moment he saw a strange glow drawing nearer to the opening of the ship's doorway. Coladeus slowly appeared, stopping right at the entrance. Coladeus scanned his surroundings, making sure he hadn't been seen by any humans.

Elt continued his silence, not sure of what to expect from the glowing creature in front of him. He was ready to lunge at the stranger. He had to protect his house, but for some reason, something kept him from attacking.

Coladeus stepped down from his ship into the yard, and slowly walked towards Elt. The glow from his body shined across the doghouse. Coladeus could see Elt's name painted over the doorway to the doghouse.

The alien was only a few feet from Elt. He knew that Elt was about to attack. Coladeus knew that he was safe. The powers he possessed were far mightier than the biggest bite of a dog. Coladeus wanted Elt to trust him, so he hoped to avoid any type of aggressions on Elt's part. Coladeus adjusted the dial on his distranulator so Elt could understand him.

"No need to be afraid, Elt," said a very calm Coladeus. "I am a friend."

Coladeus walked even closer to Elt. The dog understood the alien, but still remained on guard. The Trianthian bent down and reached out with his glowing hand so Elt could sniff it.

"I come here to ask for your help," related Coladeus.

Elt continued to stare at Coladeus, but said nothing.

"You do understand what I'm saying to you, don't you?" asked Coladeus.

Elt nodded yes.

"We're here on a peaceful mission," said Coladeus. "We understand there is trouble in your town and we are here to help."

"There is trouble," Elt replied softly. "But I don't know what's happening."

"Then we need to find out where the trouble has originated," said Coladeus. "I will need your help. That is why I landed my pod ship in your yard. I needed to meet you."

Elt moved closer to Coladeus and took a couple of really generous sniffs.

"You're definitely different from my human Ralph," said Elt. "Why do you need my help?"

"If the humans from this planet see us, then they will think that my species is trying to hurt them, not help them," replied Coladeus. "If we try to recruit an Earth being, most likely he or she wouldn't trust us. Your species, however, is much more trustworthy than the humans. We have been successful working with members of your species before."

Coladeus inched closer to Elt, his glowing body reflecting off Elt's shiny coat in the night.

"Let me formally introduce myself," Coladeus stated calmly. "I am Coladeus. I am from a planet named Trianthius, a world very far away from your world. My fellow Trianthians and I travel to many far away worlds to restore peace to countless civilizations."

"I'm supposed to protect my human's property and warn my friends if intruders come," remarked Elt.

"And you did," replied Coladeus. "You did a very commendable job. But I'm asking you to do more."

"More?" asked Elt.

"We need to find out who is behind all of the bad things going on, stop them, and restore your town back to the way it was," replied Coladeus.

"How would I do that?" asked Elt.

"Well, we'll start with this," answered Coladeus.

Coladeus reached into a pouch inside of his glowing body and pulled out the stone he had placed in his pouch when he entered the pod. He held the gem in his four-fingered hand. The gem, like his body, glowed a green light, on and then off. On and off, on and off it went.

"It's our answer to the problem," replied Coladeus. "Come closer."

Elt nudged closer to the alien. Coladeus reached over to Elt and twisted the dog's collar so that its underside was visible. Coladeus then attached the gem to the underside of the collar, and then let the collar untwist.

"It is done," declared Coladeus.

"What is done?" questioned Elt. "What did you put on me?"

"Trianthians possess certain powers," replied Coladeus. "Our powers originate from the contents in that stone. We transfer these powers, through the stone, onto living creatures like you, who then help us on our missions. There is enough power in that stone to last you one Earth year."

"Power?" asked Elt. "What kind of power?"

"In one of your Earth days, you will be able to start doing things that you could never do before," declared Coladeus. "Now you are strong, you can run fast, and leap too. But once the stone energizes you, you will run faster than any dog has ever run. You will jump much higher, and you will be very, very strong."

Coladeus rose and started walking towards his pod ship. Elt followed close behind the alien.

"You must learn how to use your new found powers correctly," stated Coladeus. "You will need to master your talents. Then you will be ready to stop the ones in your town who are causing all of the trouble."

How can I find these bad humans?" asked Elt.

"Venture out . . . . beyond your comfort zone, your neighborhood . . . . at night, when others are asleep," replied Coladeus. "Seek out information from others of your species. They may know something. With your new speed, you will get to your destinations in no time."

Coladeus climbed into his pod. He turned around to face Elt.

"Do I contact you?" asked Elt as he followed Coladeus all the way to the entrance of the pod.

"Don't worry," answered Coladeus. "Your stone contains a transmitter. I will be contacting you. I have to leave for a short time. My ship needs to leave Earth's atmosphere, or the watchers from your planet will detect us."

Coladeus turned around and sat down in his seat. Elt peered inside, and then took a brief sniff. This was all new to him.

"Remember to use your powers wisely Elt," Coladeus continued.

Elt backed away. The pod door closed. Steam flowed from the bottom of the pod, and the ship began to lift off. Once high enough, the pod ship exited quickly into the night sky.

Coming home from dinner, Ralph's dad turned his truck into the Valleydale subdivision. Staring at the night sky on Schoolhouse Road, Ralph noticed a dark shadow streak across the sky.

"What was that?" asked Ralph.

"What was what?" asked Mr. Eltison.

"It looked like something flew across the sky, but it's too dark to make anything out," replied Ralph.

"Maybe it was a bird," commented Mr. Eltison.

"Yeah, maybe it was a bird," returned Ralph. "But it must have been a big one."

Ralph and his dad drove into their driveway. Elt was outside, waiting for Ralph. Elt tried staring at the sky to see if he could pinpoint the strange pod ship and its leader, Coladeus. No luck . . . . all he could see was a brilliant array of stars and planets.

CHAPTER 9

WHEN ELT WOKE UP THE next day, he ran outside immediately. Normally, he always licked Ralph until the boy woke up, but this day was different. If Coladeus was true to his word, changes in Elt would happen. He couldn't wait.

Elt hadn't even had a chance to alert Bernadette on what had happened the night before. He would have to wait until their afternoon walk to inform her. He was excited.

"Nothing yet," said Elt to himself as he ran around the backyard. "Don't feel any different."

The effects of the Trianthian stone hadn't set in yet. Coladeus stated it would take one full Earth day for the powers to initiate.

It was Saturday, so sometimes the walks would occur earlier than normal. In fact, a three day weekend was in store for Ralph, it was Memorial Day weekend. There was no school on Monday. Ralph did have to help his dad with yard work. Although he wasn't old enough to operate the lawn mower, Ralph could rake, sweep, and dump trash.

After lunch, Ralph called Jenny, and off he went with Elt. In fact, Elt raced so hard that he pulled Ralph all the way to Jenny's house.

Not with the super strength that Coladeus had promised him, but with his own.

Elt needed time alone to talk with Bernadette, and at last he got his chance. Ralph stepped inside Jenny's house for a glass of lemonade and a snack before the walk, so both dogs were left outside for a few moments.

"I have something to tell you," explained an excited Elt. "I was visited last night by a stranger who flew down in my yard from another world."

Bernadette didn't utter a word. She just gazed at Elt strangely.

"I know it's kind of hard to believe," continued Elt. "But this being, for he's not a human, is going to help us find the bad humans who are hurting our town."

"Are you okay?" asked Bernadette. "Did your human put something in your food dish today?"

"Look, I'll prove it," declared Elt. "Watch this!"

Elt dashed to the front of Jenny's house, stopped, and then ran straight for the fence. He lunged upward, but didn't clear the fence. Elt crashed. Embarrassed from the crash, Elt hung his head in shame.

"Now you're really scaring me," said Bernadette.

"It did happen," said Elt. "He gave me special powers, right here inside my collar."

Bernadette peeked over at Elt's collar, but couldn't see anything, for the stone was attached to the inside of his collar.

"I don't see anything," said Bernadette.

At that point, the conversation ceased, Ralph and Jenny came running out of the house with their leashes. The walk was about to begin.

There were no more conversations between Elt and Bernadette that day. In fact, there was no eye contact, no sniffing, no anything. After the walk, Jenny went straight inside with her dog and Ralph headed straight home. Ralph and Jenny planned to meet at the pool later, but there were no plans to bring the pooches for the trip. Dogs weren't allowed near the pool area, but they could walk or run in all other areas of the park.

Elt and Bernadette didn't really have time to finish their talk. That was probably good for Elt, he had just made himself look pretty foolish with all of that special powers nonsense he was feeding her.

Ralph came home from swimming around dinner time. Elt laid in his bed for the rest of the day, waiting for his human to come home. On one of his trips outside, Elt did try to run around and once again to test out his new powers, but again, everything was still the same. He didn't try to jump the fence again. He was a little weary about crashing.

Night fell on that day like any other. Ralph was exhausted from all the swimming he had done earlier. He played a little with Elt before retiring to his bed. A quick bath and a snack was all Ralph needed to fall fast asleep.

Later that night, Elt walked around the house to make sure everything was safe. He then stayed under the dining room table for awhile before returning back to bed with Ralph. Once he was settled and just about ready to fall asleep, Elt heard a voice.

"Elt! Elt! Can you hear me?" asked the voice.

Elt opened his eyes and gazed around the room.

"Elt, can you hear me?" the voice asked again. "This is Coladeus. I visited you last night. I'm communicating to you through the transmitter in the stone."

Now understanding what was happening, Elt moved to the living room so he could communicate with Coladeus without waking anyone up. Mr. Eltison was in his room reading and Ralph was still sleeping.

"I hear you," responded Elt.

"Good," replied Coladeus. "You need to go outside."

Elt exited the doggie door and stared at all of the stars in the sky. The backyard was totally dark, except for a faint light coming from the kitchen.

"Okay, I'm outside," said Elt.

"Good," returned Coladeus. "Now I want you to start running towards your front yard fence, and don't stop until you've leaped over it."

Elt was hesitant about obeying Coladeus's command.

"Oh, I tried that earlier today and it didn't work so well," returned Elt.

"Your transformation wasn't complete," said Coladeus. "You needed one full Earth day."

"Here goes nothing," said Elt to himself.

Elt backed up to his doghouse, took a deep breath, and then ran with all his might towards the fence. His speed had increased, and before he knew it, was right in front of the fence. Elt sprang back with his hind legs and easily cleared the chain-linked fence.

"Wow!" exclaimed Elt. "I did it!"

"Excellent," responded Coladeus. "In time, you will learn to control your powers, so you don't become the center of attention."

Elt nodded in agreement. He glanced at the fence he just easily cleared, then down at his legs. Jenny's fence was the same height, so clearly Elt just needed more time. Now he needed to still convince Bernadette about the whole super powers thing.

Coladeus's words were true. The stranger had told Elt the truth. What new strengths was he going to receive? What was he going to do with these new powers?

"Now run down the street as fast as you can," commanded Coladeus over the transmitter.

Elt obeyed, taking off from Springhaven Court and continuing onto Valleydale Drive and back home in mere seconds. He halted right in front of the house. Elt wasn't breathing heavy at all.

"I trust you are happy with your speed?" asked Coladeus.

"I'm like really fast!" blurted Elt.

"One more task for you tonight, my friend," stated Coladeus. "Hop over your fence, and run towards the front of your house, and jump."

Elt followed Coladeus's instructions again. He easily hopped over the fence. He ran to the house and leaped. Before he knew it, Elt had landed on the roof of the house. Another amazing feat had been accomplished! Gazing down at the ground below him, Elt hopped up and down along the slightly slanted rooftop.

"I suppose you made it to the top of your house by now," stated Coladeus calmly. "We're done for the night. Get some rest. I will contact you within the next two Earth days. Good night Elt."

"Wait! Wait!" exclaimed Elt. "When can I go fight the bad humans? Hello?"

The transmission between Elt and Coladeus had concluded. The alien didn't answer back. However, someone else answered.

"How are you going to get back down?" asked a familiar voice to Elt.

Out of the night's shadows and into Elt's yard, Jasmine appeared.

"Quite impressive," Jasmine commented. "I thought I could really jump high, but you . . . . you are really special. What is your human feeding you that can make you jump so high?"

"Uh . . . . Hi Jasmine," said Elt. "What are you doing up so late at night?"

"Duh . . . . I'm a cat, remember?" Jasmine replied. "I practically stay up all night. My question is, what are you doing up so late at night?"

"Gee, I guess I need to explain some things," returned Elt. "Can we call an emergency meeting?"

"Well, I guess I can give Sarge a visit tomorrow," replied Jasmine. "What's this all about?"

Elt jumped to the ground. Jasmine couldn't believe what she had just witnessed.

"I think we can stop the bad things that are happening," said Elt. "But I'm gonna need help."

"You're going to find out what's going on?" asked Jasmine. "So far our neighborhood is safe."

"Yeah, but if we don't do something about it now, things will get worse everywhere," answered Elt.

"I'll let you know when we can meet at Juan's place," said Jasmine.

The feline walked off, jumped onto her fence, and the disappeared into her yard. The stars in the night sky seemed to shimmer down on Elt, like a spotlight on a Hollywood movie star. Now Elt realized that something special was happening to him.

The only issue was that he was supposed to keep his special powers a secret. Elt had already tried to tell Bernadette, and now Jasmine knew something was going on with him. In Elt's mind though, Coladeus wouldn't be disappointed in him as long as he kept his secret away from humans. He couldn't show off any of his powers to Ralph, Ralph's dad, or any human, a human would think it rather odd that an animal, especially a domestic pet like Elt, could run so fast and leap all the way to the roof of a house.

He made up his mind as whether or not to show Bernadette his powers. He had made a fool of himself earlier that day, but was quite confident that the next time would be totally different. He would see her soon. Sometimes on Sundays they wouldn't do walks, so that was one less chance of speaking to her, but what about the emergency meeting? He would hopefully see her then. Would Bernadette believe him?

Elt made his way inside. He was very excited about the night's events. He had trouble sleeping. Finally, after about an hour, Elt rested his head next to Ralph's and fell asleep.

The morning came with Elt still asleep and Ralph awake. In fact, Ralph had to wake his dog up that morning.

Sunday was a special day. On that day, the day before Memorial Day, Spring Valley ushered in the beginning of summer with a big town-wide picnic at the city park. With the pool open, the lake ready for boating, and all other outdoor events, it was customary for families in Spring Valley to get together.

Now for all the negative events that had been going on lately in the town, the folks of Spring Valley ventured out and celebrated the beginning of hopefully an improved summer. The efforts of Crum and his men, although no one knew that these men were behind all of the negative events, were not going to dampen the spirits that weekend. But there was still that uneasiness of "something might happen."

Pets were included in the celebration, especially dogs. Folks were allowed to bring their dogs to the park that day, on a leash of course. It was a great chance for dogs and humans to have fun together.

That was perfect for Elt. Other than the venture to Juan's place, his daily walks, and the trip to the vet's office, Elt had never traveled anywhere else before. Elt was excited, although he wasn't sure where he was going. But he saw Ralph's dad pack items in the car and Ralph carrying a leash. Elt knew that wherever the humans were going that day, chances are he was going too.

Ralph, his dad, and Elt stepped into the truck. Elt paid close attention on how exactly they traveled to the park. Elt knew that he would probably have to travel that way again on one of his nightly trips to scope out the town. He'd have to make sure and remember the way there and back.

A right on Valleydale, a right on Schoolhouse, and then a left on Pleasant Grove took them to the park. After Mr. Eltison parked the truck, Ralph, his dad, and Elt unpacked the truck and headed towards the lake. They brought lawn chairs, a blanket, a baseball, a couple of baseball gloves, a bat, and a cooler full of juices, sodas, and sandwiches.

A few cats were there at the park, but they remained in their pet carriers. One kid brought his small hamster cage while a little girl brought her pet pig to the park, on a leash of course.

There were softball games, rowboats on the lake, swimming in both the lake and at the pool, and the tennis court was full. There were Frisbee games for the humans to play with their dogs. Some dogs could jump pretty high to fetch the Frisbee in mid-air. Elt wanted to join in, but was afraid that if he did participate, he would easily out-jump any other dog, which then would attract quite a bit of attention by the humans. Elt decided to pay no attention to the games.

Elt's patience paid off. While Ralph and his dad were throwing the baseball to each other, Elt was lying under a tree watching them. He spotted Jenny, her mom, and Bernadette walking towards Ralph and his dad.

"Hi, nice to meet you," greeted Mr. Eltison. "I'm Paul Eltison."

"Pleasure meeting you," returned Jenny's mom. "I'm Wendy Rodgers."

While the parents exchanged conversation, Ralph and Jenny talked for a few moments, and then threw the baseball to each other. The interaction between the kids gave Elt just enough time to communicate with Bernadette. Jenny's dog sat beside Elt.

"I'm glad you came," said Elt. "I have some important things to tell you."

"What's up?" asked Bernadette.

"Well, it's about yesterday, when I tried showing you the special powers I received from Coladeus."

"Oh, you're not talking about that again?" Bernadette returned.

"It's true, it happened to me last night," said Elt. "Jasmine was there, she saw me do some amazing things."

"What exactly can you do?" Bernadette asked.

"Run very fast, leap, maybe even fly some," answered Elt. "I'm not sure how strong I am though."

"And how did you obtain these powers again?" Bernadette asked.

She knew the answer, but she wanted to hear it again just to make sure.

"From a being, not a human, from another world," said Elt. "His name is Coladeus. He placed this tiny pebble on my collar, well on the inside, well you remember me telling you yesterday. You do believe me, don't you?"

"I want to believe you," replied Bernadette. "But what you're saying is very hard to believe, and you know what happened yesterday when you attempted to leap my human's fence."

"I'll have to show you," said Elt. "Jasmine is calling a special meeting. As soon as she lets us know, we'll be meeting at Juan's place again."

The conversation ended there, for Ralph and Jenny ran over to Elt and Bernadette. The kids went for a long walk in the park. After the walk, Ralph, Jenny, and their parents settled in for a picnic lunch. Ralph's dad and Jenny's mom decided to combine their blankets and share their lunches.

The two families sat under a score of shade trees along with many other families. They ate sandwiches, potato salad, coleslaw, chips, fruit, and pudding for dessert. Elt and Bernadette received uneaten sandwich corners from Ralph and Jenny. Some of the families took advantage of the barbecue pits that were positioned in the park. They cooked hotdogs, hamburgers, and even steaks on the grill.

The day's cheeriness was about to change. While Ralph, Jenny, their parents, and the pooches were casually eating their lunches, they were approached by a couple of strange visitors.

"Excuse me sir and madam," said the polite yet dark voice. "We have come today to ask folks here if they would be interested in selling their homes to us, real fast if you know what I mean?"

That was no ordinary voice, but a voice that very few in town knew. These were no two ordinary men, but two of Mr. Crum's devious agents, Frake and his brother Jake.

"We represent W.E.C. Insurance," continued Frake. "We have an office downtown on Main Street. With all the unfortunate events going on here lately, we've had quite a few folks decide that they wanted to sell their homes and re-locate."

"I'm sorry, but I'm not interested," replied Mr. Eltison.

Ralph's dad glanced over at Jenny's mom. She nodded her head in agreement.

"Me neither, but thank you," said Mrs. Rodgers.

"Very well," said Frake calmly. "If you change your minds, please give us a call."

Frake handed Mr. Eltison one of his business cards, and then moved onto the next set of families. Both Elt and Bernadette did not like the looks of Frake and his brother. Their growls were low, but Frake noticed Elt, who was ready to pounce on him if anything happened to his human.

Something was not right about those two humans. Elt had no idea if those two characters were the cause of all the town's mishaps, but sensed something was up with them, and it wasn't good at all. He would have to keep an eye on those two, especially if he ever saw them again, and report his findings to Coladeus.

The rest of the day and evening was pleasant for Ralph, his dad, and Elt. After they left the picnic, Ralph spent the rest of the day messing around in his room and watching some television with his dad. Elt took a long nap on his bed. After dinner, Ralph and Elt played in the backyard.

At night, after all the humans were asleep, Elt ventured outside. He hoped he would receive some kind of message from Coladeus, but the message he did receive was from his friend and neighbor, Jasmine the feline.

"We will meet at Juan's on the second day of the sun after tonight, when the sun is all the way above us, like last time," Jasmine reported to Elt.

So Elt was to meet at mid-day on the second day, which was Tuesday, the day after Memorial Day. Elt accepted the message and Jasmine ran off to chase rabbits that were in her yard.

Memorial Day arrived and left, with Ralph going swimming for a few hours with Jenny and a couple of her friends at the pool on Schoolhouse Road. Elt stayed home with Ralph's dad, who finished some chores around the house.

The day after Memorial Day, a school day and work day for most, was the day that the neighborhood pets of the Valleydale subdivision would hold their emergency meeting around noon, when the sun was at its highest peak of the day. Elt had practiced some of the extraordinary feats the night before while everyone in his house was asleep. Everything he accomplished a couple of nights before he accomplished again. Running, jumping, and even leaping on and off the roof again were some of the exercises he performed. Elt wanted to make sure that he was still the powerful pooch that Coladeus told him he would be. The day of the meeting was no day to lose his powers.

"I want to try one more thing," Elt announced to Jasmine that night. She sat perched on the fence, facing Elt's front yard.

Elt raced to the backyard. Jasmine followed him. Behind the weeping willow tree, there was an old log from a tree that used to stand in the yard, but had fallen during a wind storm years ago. Ralph's dad had planned on using the log as a landscape timber in a flower bed.

Elt walked up to the log, nudged his snout underneath it, and easily moved the over two-hundred pound piece of timber. Then Elt thought of another idea. He gripped onto one of the ends of the log with his teeth, grabbed a firm hold of it, and then raised the log into the air.

"And just how did you learn how to do that?" asked an astonished Jasmine. "Jumping, running, and picking up heavy items. And that thing you do on and off the roof. I don't know how you do it, but it's something special."

Elt dropped the log onto the ground.

"If I told you the truth right now, you wouldn't believe it," mentioned Elt. "But at the meeting, I will tell you all the truth about what has happened to me."

After a few moments of small talk, Jasmine left Elt. Staring at the stars for awhile and waiting for a transmission from Coladeus, Elt finally walked back inside. He quietly fell asleep, and awaited the next day's meeting with his fellow neighborhood pets.

CHAPTER 10

"SO WHAT'S SO IMPORTANT THAT we have to call a special meeting?" asked Sarge as he picked through the bowl of tasty treats that Juan had placed in a bowl that morning. "Although I don't mind coming out to taste these delicious biscuits, emergency meetings are for you know, emergencies."

Elt had arrived again with Bernadette for the meeting, just like the time before.

"I called the meeting today," declared Elt. He stepped in front of the others.

In attendance besides Elt and Bernadette were Sarge, Juan, Chin, Max, and Jasmine.

"Tell us what's on your mind kid," said Max.

"Well, I know who can stop all the bad things from happening in our town," said Elt.

"Who?" asked Juan.

"Well," paused Elt, "me, with your help, of course."

The pets stared at each other. They looked more confused than ever.

"How can we help stop the bad humans?" asked Sarge. "Other than protecting our human's house, I don't know what we can do. And what can you do? You're just a pup."

Sarge was right, well in his mind he thought he was right. What could this young squirt of a pup do?

"I was given powers, special powers," insisted Elt. "These powers will help us catch the bad humans."

"Oh no, not that again," Bernadette interjected.

Jasmine jumped off the rafters onto a row of boxes.

"Elt, just show them," Jasmine said. "It's too hard to explain."

Elt searched around the garage and found an old heavy chest that was just a few feet from the group. He walked over to it.

"Sarge, could you please try and move this?" asked Elt.

With all of his might, the Boxer growled and snarled, huffed and puffed, but couldn't budge the heavy chest.

"Must not have gotten enough sleep last night," commented Sarge as he moved out of the way. He would have never moved that chest, but making that clever excuse made him feel better.

Elt moved closer to the chest, clutched onto its handle with his teeth, and easily dragged the heavy chest across the floor. Then, like a bolt of lightning, darted all around the room, jumping from wall to wall. The dogs and Jasmine couldn't keep up with Elt's every move, for the pooch was moving way too fast. Bernadette couldn't believe it. Her eyes watched Elt and his every move.

"Good gracious," gawked Max. "What has that boy been eating?"

Elt jumped down from the rafters in front of his friends. Bernadette walked up to him, still in shock.

"I guess I owe you an apology," remarked Bernadette. "But are you still going to tell us that beings from outer space gave you these powers?"

"Outer space?" asked Max.

Elt chuckled, and then jumped up on top of the chest. The other dogs once again fixed their attention to the young dog.

"Soon I will be going out at night," said Elt. "I will search for their hiding place. I will definitely need your help."

"I'm sticking around here and protecting my human's house!" commanded Sarge. "Nothing else!"

"Listen to what the boy has to say," said Max. "If we go with Elt's plan, then maybe we won't have to worry about the bad humans coming here."

"Exactly!" added Jasmine.

Sarge wasn't happy. It wasn't just the fact that he was wrong and Elt was right. It was more that this young pup was running the show and making the plans. He was supposed to be in charge. This was his neighborhood. Challenging Elt to a duel would be foolish, he had just witnessed this pup doing things he had never seen a human or any animal do. Sarge just shrugged and wandered over to the biscuit bowl, where he fetched one more dog biscuit.

"Then it's decided," interjected Max.

"I'm awaiting instructions," said Elt. "As soon as I hear from . . . . you know . . . . the beings . . . . well they're called Trianthians, I will let you know."

It was that time of the meeting again. Everyone waited for Chin to close out the meeting with one of his famous proverbs. The Chow Chow scratched his neck for a few seconds, and then uttered "You can't make peanut butter and jelly sandwich without jelly."

Then Chin promptly bid everyone adieu and walked out the door. For a moment the pets sat and contemplated Chin's words. At first, Chin's statement didn't make any sense, which was usually par for the course.

Then it all became clearer. In order to make a "pb and j" sandwich, you need both peanut butter and jelly. What Chin was trying to say was that the pup Elt and the neighborhood pets needed to work as a team in order to make their mission successful. You needed both peanut butter and jelly, not just peanut butter. Elt, even with his newly found powers, needed help from pets he could trust. The team had to find the root of the problem, get rid of it, and help restore Spring Valley's good name.

That was how the meeting adjourned. The walk home was quiet for Elt and Bernadette. Bernadette felt ashamed for not believing in Elt. To believe that a being from outer space granted your best friend extraordinary powers was tough. Elt wasn't upset. He understood why Bernadette had been so skeptical.

Nightfall arrived, and with it, finally a message from Coladeus. It had been a few days since the last message, but Elt had been patient.

The Trianthian could only contact his mediums when Trianthius I was in range of the medium's home planet.

Coladeus's message was simple that night. Go out past the neighborhood, without being detected of course, and see if he could spot anything suspicious. Lastly, report anything suspicious.

The message seemed simple enough, and it was a good start. In order to find anything, Elt would have to go beyond the perimeters of where he lived, because nothing had yet happened in his neighborhood.

Elt easily leaped over his fence and headed down Springhaven, Valleydale, and up towards Schoolhouse Road. He wasn't alone, though. Jasmine appeared from behind Elt. She had made her way to Schoolhouse Road a few minutes earlier, she knew she was never going to keep up with her friend. So she took off early and hoped that Elt would show.

"You need some assistance?" she asked. "A cat has nothing to do on a night like this and I'm tired of chasing rabbits."

"Sure," replied Elt. "Just try and stay hidden. If you can't catch up, just hop on my back and I will carry you."

"I'm a cat," said Jasmine. "One of my specialties is staying hidden."

Elt and Jasmine headed to the city park, the place Elt was just a few days ago. Elt searched all around the lake, while Jasmine checked out the pool and picnic shelters. There was nothing suspicious in the park. It was very quiet.

On the way home, Jasmine rode on Elt's back so they could get home faster. He would report his findings, which was nothing, the next time Coladeus called him.

The next day's news was grim. Like every morning, Elt delivered the morning newspaper to Mr. Eltison at the kitchen table. Elt couldn't read the words on the newspaper. All he had to do was read the expressions on Mr. Eltison's face.

There was another burglary in Spring Valley. There were more houses for sale and new ones for rent. Elt had patrolled one part of town, and everything was fine. He must have been in the wrong place. He would have to go out again.

As bad news spread around town, so did news from dog to dog and cat to cat. In Elt's neighborhood, it was more like dog to dog and cat to dog. Even during the day, barks were being heard for miles, transferring messages from one dog to another about what to do next. There weren't any answers, but many questions like "What are we going to do?" and "Who's doing this, why, and when will it stop?"

Without any news or commands from Coladeus, Elt decided to go out again that night. He didn't take Jasmine along. Although he enjoyed the company and Jasmine stayed well hidden, Elt was much faster and he didn't have to carry her for the whole trip.

Elt headed towards the park again on Pleasant Grove Road, but instead of taking a right to the park, he took a left and headed uptown, where he heard through the far-off barks of other canines that terrible things had occurred at the Spring Valley Shopping Center. Elt would have to be careful. He knew he could outrun any human, he just didn't want to be seen. Elt kept close to the trees that lined the road. It was late, so most of the stores in the shopping center were closed, except for the gas station and the grocery store.

When there were no cars passing by, Elt raced across the street and hid behind the garbage dumpster. He watched a couple of cars that stopped in front of the gas pumps. After a few moments, Elt turned his attention to the grocery store. Elt hid between a couple of parked cars and watched as the grocery store manager closed the doors at midnight without incident.

It was getting late, so Elt decided to head back. Even though he was granted these special powers, he still had to rely on his sniffing senses to get back home. Once back on Schoolhouse Road, Elt knew he was on his way home. He soon arrived in his own yard.

Although he didn't find anything suspicious on his first two missions, Elt was feeling confident about knowing his way around town. When he was about to walk inside, Coladeus contacted him. Elt reported where he had traveled the last couple of nights. Coladeus wasn't disappointed at all. All the Trianthian leader said was "keep up the hard work until hopefully he will find a clue." Elt felt winded from the trip. He fell fast asleep once he crept into bed with Ralph.

The next evening when Elt left his yard, he headed right on Schoolhouse Road to Pleasant Grove Road, and then another right to downtown. All was quiet that night. After an hour of inactivity, Elt traveled back home.

The next few evenings followed the same pattern. Elt would either venture uptown or downtown, but he couldn't find anything out of the ordinary. There were no clues, or maybe there were, and he just wasn't experienced enough to find them. Why couldn't he find anything? He was wondering if the trouble was really originating in town.

After reporting minimal activity to Coladeus, the Trianthian leader developed a plan to utilize alien technology to assist Elt. The aliens used the same devices that took photo images of Elt. Focusing on the busiest districts in Spring Valley, Matheun photographed numerous camera shots of the town. He took photos of humans, places, and objects. One big drawback was that Matheun could only take day photos, night photos were too dark to obtain any visible images. Coladeus would still have to rely on Elt.

"We're bound to run into something sooner or later," commented Coladeus to Elt.

Although he didn't know it at the time, Coladeus was correct indeed. It was a very good idea to continue his nightly trips, luck was about to turn in their favor.

On the next evening out, Elt journeyed again downtown. He stopped close to Drexel's, his old home before he became Ralph's pet. He didn't remember it, but something about the smell of that place was familiar.

After taking another sniff of the area, Elt witnessed his first clue. A car pulled into an alley behind the W.E.C. Insurance building. Elt decided to investigate. The car stopped, two men got out of the car, and opened the back door of the building. The car's headlights remained lit, so the two men could easily be recognized.

Elt had seen these two humans before. He knew he was onto something. One man opened the trunk, while the other grabbed a cart from inside the building. They both started loading items into the cart and then pushed the cart back into the building. For some reason, maybe just a plain old bad habit, the last man who entered didn't shut the door completely. That was Elt's chance to take a closer look.

Elt quickly dashed through the back alley and stopped at the back entrance of the building. He peeked inside cautiously, not to be noticed by the two men who had just entered the structure. He sneaked inside.

The first room Elt entered was dark, but it led to a room that was well lit. Hidden by a stack of boxes in the dark room, Elt had a clear view of what was going on in the next room. The two men were loading money and other valuables into their huge safe. Elt, being a dog, didn't really know what they were loading was stolen, but he sensed that these fellows were up to no good.

Now Elt had a better glimpse of one of the two men as he turned around. Like he sensed before, Elt knew the human, he saw him just about a week or so ago at the park. The man had approached Ralph's dad and Jenny's mom. It was Frake, the human that he and Bernadette didn't like, and his senses offered no difference in opinion the second time he saw him.

Frake was joined by his brother Jake. From another room, Bull walked in. The three men sat down and started eating. From his view in the dark room, Elt tried to spot anything else that was suspicious.

Luck had been on Elt's side that night, as he finally spotted something that was not right, and he successfully entered the hideout without being noticed. As fate would have it, sooner or later, luck was about to change. All of a sudden, Elt's collar spoke to him. It was Coladeus.

"Elt, where are you?" asked Coladeus.

The message wasn't very loud, but loud enough for the men to hear. Even with their noisy, disgusting eating habits, the three men could still hear something originating from the back room. Fortunately, Coladeus was speaking "dog speak," so the message was garbled for humans.

Frake wiped his mouth on his sleeve and sat up. Elt didn't know what to do, so like any other animal he froze, and stayed hidden behind the boxes. Super speed and strength could help him escape trouble, but Elt was inexperienced, and didn't know exactly what he should do next.

Frake turned on the light to the previously dark room. Elt dashed out from the boxes and growled at him. When Frake reached over to grab Elt, the dog easily pushed over the boxes. The stack of boxes fell on Frake and Elt sped out the back door. He didn't stop until he reached his back porch of his home on Springhaven Court.

Jake and Bull jumped out of their chairs when they heard the ruckus. The two men started moving boxes out of Frake's way.

"Who was that?" asked Jake.

Frake pulled himself off the ground.

"A dog," replied Frake.

Bull ran to the back door and stuck his head out of the back entrance. He didn't see anything in the back alley.

As Elt remembered who Frake was, Crum's top man remembered Elt.

"I've seen that dog before," continued Frake as he straightened himself.

"Whoever and wherever he is, he's not coming back here tonight," said Bull.

Bull shut the back door. The men walked back into the room to finish their meals.

CHAPTER 11

RRRRING!!! THE SCHOOL BELL RANG for the last time of the school year. Ralph, Jenny, and the rest of their schoolmates cheered their way down the halls, saying good-bye to all their teachers until their late summer return to the fifth grade.

It was mid-June. The pleasant sunny days of May turned into the hot steamy days of June. Although Memorial Day traditionally marked the summer's beginning, school summer vacation meant the real start of summer for most of the kids and teachers.

Not much of Ralph's daily routines changed in the summer, except for the obvious fact that he didn't have to attend school. His dad worked at home, so Ralph didn't need a sitter or have to visit a summer day camp. If Ralph's dad had to leave for awhile, he simply had his son tag along with him. Ralph enjoyed the road trips with his dad, even if they were mainly in town and to places he had visited before.

Jenny Rodgers, however, had a few changes to deal with. On the last day of school, Jenny came home as usual and her mom was home, her mom usually left her office in time to be home before Jenny returned from school.

Jenny's mom worked at an office downtown on the corner of Maple and First Streets. She, like Mr. Eltison, was a single parent. Jenny's mom had to make sure that she was home in time for Jenny's arrival from school. If Wendy Rodgers had to stay late, she would get a friend to watch Jenny, or have a grandparent who lived close by to do the same.

Now that school was out, Wendy Rodgers still had to work, and there was no one to watch Jenny all day while she was gone. Ms. Rodger's only choice was to let Jenny stay with her grandparents in the morning. Jenny's grandparents lived uptown, near the Spring Valley Shopping Center. Ms. Rodgers worked a little later during the summer, because she had appropriate day care. If she left work by five o'clock, Wendy would pick Jenny up and drive home. If she stayed even later, Jenny would just spend the night with her grandparents.

What was the significance of all that? First, Jenny was Ralph's best friend. She wasn't a girlfriend, but more like a real good friend that Ralph enjoyed spending time with. Likewise, Jenny enjoyed spending time with Ralph. Ralph and Jenny spent a great deal of time together, whether it was time swimming or hanging out, or going on their daily walks together with Elt and Bernadette.

Less time together between the two children meant less time for walks with the pets, which meant less time for Elt and Bernadette. Sometimes they would have walks together after dinner, the daylight was longer and there was still time for a walk. But there were times that there were no walks at all. Elt and Bernadette didn't understand why they didn't go on their usual walks. It was just something dogs didn't understand.

Meeting Bernadette daily was very important for Elt, since there were clues now for the cause of all the terrible events going on in the town, plus he really enjoyed her company. Elt needed to relate Coladeus's instructions to Bernadette and the other neighborhood dogs. Elt had to rely on howls and barks at night, or send Jasmine to Sarge, Juan, and Max with an important message.

Elt had indeed discovered a key clue that night. As he was running home that night from his confrontation with Frake, Elt thought about what he witnessed. The two men loading stuff out of the back of their car and placing it all in that giant metal box. The biggest fact of it all was the sense of uneasiness that Elt felt when he saw Frake, the same sense he felt when he was at the picnic. He knew something smelled rotten.

"Elt, are you okay?" asked Coladeus. Once again Coladeus was trying to reach Elt.

Elt heard the message just as he leaped over his fence into the yard. Elt responded. He informed Coladeus about the evening's events and how he had met the stranger before at the park. Coladeus was pleased. Elt's message and wealth of information ignited a spark in the Trianthian leader's quest to neutralize the bad humans.

When Elt didn't answer earlier in the evening, the Trianthians sensed that there may have been trouble. They tracked Elt's exact location through the gem on his collar.

At that time, Matheun pulled up pictures of the exact spot Elt was when he didn't answer his first transmission. With the use of their technology, similar to that of an x-ray machine, Mathuen was able to photograph the inside of the W.E.C. Insurance building, for the rooms were bright enough for Matheun to take a clear picture. Matheun witnessed a safe overflowing with money, jewels, and other valuables. That was all Coladeus and his crew needed to see. Dogs may not know what money was, but Trianthians knew. Coldeus knew now that Elt had hit a jackpot of clues.

Matheun pushed more buttons. New images popped up before them.

"W.E.C. are the initials on the structure windows," reported Matheun. "When I feed these letters into our processor, the only name I come up with is that of a Walter Eugene Crum, President and CEO of Bordertown Bank and Trust Company."

"Bordertown . . . . Bordertown," Coladeus repeated to himself. "That's it! Our initial report was that something in Bordertown might be the cause of all the conflicts in Spring Valley. Matheun, let's process more information on this Walter Eugene Crum."

The information was endless. Crum was a rich businessman, richer than rich. He was a harsh landlord and a man who basically owned Bordertown.

"If he originated from Bordertown, why would he choose to move to Spring Valley?" asked Matheun. Coladeus thought for a moment. It didn't take too long for Coladeus to figure it out.

"To spread evil and terror," answered Coladeus. "Crum wants to expand his empire. We've seen this many times before in our travels, haven't we?"

"Yes Captain," Matheun answered.

Coladeus rose from his seat while a procession of Crum's images flashed in front of him. Shortly after, pictures of Frake and his cohorts were presented to Coladeus.

"I don't see any pictures of Crum with these men," mentioned Matheun.

"And you probably won't," returned Coladeus. "These men are carrying out his diabolical plan."

"Coladeus, will this mission be a difficult one?" asked Matheun.

"I don't think so," replied Coladeus. "We've toppled dictators, stopped ruthless armies, and now we're going to hit these characters where it hurts. Zero in on that large container filled with all the treasures."

Matheun directed his computer to zoom in on the valuables that were in the safe. It held countless stacks of wrapped cash, jewelry, and other valuables.

"We're going to need Elt to take from them what they took from Spring Valley," stated Coladeus.

That was the plan, and the order that was going to be given to Elt. The super dog was instructed to take all the cash and valuables from the safe and return it somehow to the community. Stealing was wrong, but not the way they were going to do it. Coladeus didn't desire the valuables for himself; he wanted to make sure it got back to its owners. Without all that money in the safe, Frake and his men wouldn't have the extra cash needed to pay for all that real estate they wanted.

The plan was set for a late night in Mid-June. While Ralph and his dad were fast asleep, Elt went to work. This time he recruited Jasmine. Also, Elt welcomed a new partner for a mission . . . . Bernadette.

Through the use of the Rodger's new doggie door that had just been installed, Bernadette had easy access in and out of her house. Elt and Jasmine met outside his yard. Then they stopped by Bernadette's house. She was already waiting for them patiently by her front gate. Elt easily nudged her front gate open.

Now Elt was too fast for his friends Jasmine and Bernadette. Even his walk was more like a very fast trot to the other two. Elt had to be reminded a couple of times to slow down and let them catch up.

"I forget sometimes," commented Elt as they journeyed down Pleasant Grove Road.

Once the three were downtown, they stopped at Feldman's Hardware Store. Mr. Feldman had been a victim of two burglaries in the recent months, but what Elt was about to do wasn't burglary. Mr. Feldman was about to get his property back; to do that Elt would need a certain piece of equipment to complete the mission.

In front of the hardware store outside were various tools, lawnmowers, wheel barrels, grass seed, and fertilizer. Nestled in between the shovels and the wheel barrels were a couple of red wagons that were chained to a pole that supported the storefront canopy.

Coladeus could track Elt's progress through the tracking device in his transmitter that was on his collar. If Elt ran into trouble, Coladeus could assist Elt by communicating with his medium.

Elt gripped the chain that secured the wagon between his teeth. The chain easily snapped. Elt also nabbed a steel bar that was lying up against the front wall. Jasmine kept her eyes open for any humans, including Deputy Taylor, who was now working nights because of all the crime that had overcome Spring Valley.

Elt pulled the wagon across the street and stopped in the back alley behind the W.E.C. Insurance building.

"Now we wait," called Coladeus's voice to Elt.

Bernadette and Elt waited by the wagon. It was parked just beyond view in the alley. Jasmine slipped inside the wagon and laid down for a short rest.

Frake's car was parked by the back door. No one knew if those guys were going to leave that night, but Coladeus and Elt were counting on it in order to complete the mission.

After about an hour, luck was on their side, suddenly the back door opened, the three men exited, got in the car, and drove off. It was time for the three pets to make their move.

Elt wheeled the wagon over to the back door. With part of the steel rod in his mouth, Elt easily wedged the back door open with his super strength. Once inside, Elt had to accomplish one more spectacular feat . . . . he had to break open that humongous steel safe.

Dynamite was usually the only solution, but most thieves never owned a dog with super strength to assist them in opening the safe. It took a few minutes more than Elt expected, but once again Elt utilized the steel rod to pry the door open. In fact, the steel rod was so bent after Elt's second use he would have to bend it back in shape again if he ever needed to use it.

Once the safe door was opened, it was time for all three to clean it out. Elt, Bernadette, and Jasmine started grabbing stacks of money and pieces of jewelry. Using their mouths and paws, they neatly and quickly loaded the merchandise in the wagon. Bernadette found a few duffel bags that made the job easier.

Within a few minutes, the safe was empty and the wagon was stock full of money and valuables. Elt carefully tugged on the wagon. With Jasmine in front of the wagon and Bernadette behind, Elt rolled the wagon through the alley, and onto Main Street. They stopped on First Street, right in front of the Spring Valley Police Department, per Coladeus's instructions. They left the wagon right at the station's doorsteps. Not wanting to be noticed, Elt, Bernadette, and Jasmine darted off into the darkness.

Once Elt's mission was completed, Matheun pushed a couple of buttons on his computer, and a quick call to Sheriff Thomas was made. The unidentified, computerized voice informed the sheriff that he needed to get to the station as soon as possible; that something was left for him in front of the station.

Within a few minutes, Deputy Taylor's cruiser arrived. He discovered a big red wagon chock full of money, jewelry, and other valuables. Where did that come from? How did it get there? The deputy was mystified.

The mission, which was Elt's most imperative, was a huge monumental success! Elt and his friends had retrieved Spring Valley National Bank's money and more, much more. In the morning, phone calls would be made to whoever had their belongings stolen in the last few months. Chances were that folks would get some money back.

The confused and horrific look on Frake's face was indescribable. He and his two men had only left their hideout for about an hour to plan their next evil deed. When they returned, their back door was wedged open and their huge safe was empty. Frake bent down to inspect the safe. Everything they had stolen was stolen from them.

"Mr. Crum isn't going to like this," uttered Bull.

"How did they get in?" asked Jake. "Not a trace of explosives in sight. Only someone with super human strength could tear the door off that safe."

While Frake was still bent down in the safe, he shined his flashlight in every corner of the empty safe. Lying in the corner was a hair. Not of a human, but most likely an animal. He mashed his thumb down on the floor of the safe and the hair stuck to his thumb. Frake examined the hair closely.

"Who could have done this?" asked Bull.

Frake paused for a moment as he continued his examination. He held the hair close to his nose and took a sniff.

"Don't know yet," answered Frake. "But I have a feeling that what happened the other night has something to do with it."

Frake had no idea who Elt was, but now he knew that the confrontation he had with him a few nights ago was no coincidence. Now a hair popping up, a hair most likely belonging to a dog, he knew somehow that dog was involved.

"We'll call Mr. Crum in the morning," said Frake. "We all know how he hates to be awakened at night. Keep an eye out for that dog we saw the other night."

Jake and Bull shook their heads in approval. They continued to comb the room for more clues.

News spread fast of the humongous pile of money and goods that were left at the police station. STOLEN MONEY RETURNED was the headline in the Herald's morning special edition. A free copy was delivered to every citizen.

Bank officials matched most of the money returned as theirs, for the serial numbers matched the bank records before the robbery. Mrs. Simon was delighted to say the least. A great deal of money that had been stolen was back in the bank's safe.

The rest of the returned items were divided amongst all the businesses and citizens that had been robbed or burglarized. Folks were happy with what they received, for they figured that their stolen treasures were gone for good.

When Frake and his men walked to Brown's the next morning for a cup of coffee, they noticed a big crowd gathered around the front steps of the police station. They walked over and witnessed a jubilant

Mayor Helms joyfully speaking to his citizens. The men heard the news about the stolen items being returned to the police station.

Frake just turned around and headed for Brown's. They were powerless. The money and goods they had stolen were never really theirs, so they couldn't claim it. Mr. Crum would visit in a day or two to meet with them and assess the damages and how it would affect their overall plan.

The citizens of Spring Valley were ecstatic. Someone had returned the stolen property that was theirs. The desperation, worry, and sadness had disappeared from their faces as they passed each other downtown or at the grocery store.

Elt, Bernadette, and Jasmine returned the evening of their mission exhausted. Bernadette dashed inside and flopped down on her living room floor. Jasmine rested on her front porch. Elt made it to Ralph's bed and was almost asleep when he heard Coladeus calling him.

Coldeus congratulated Elt on a job well done. He reminded Elt that the fight against these bad humans wasn't over, but they had won a very pivotal battle. Coladeus told Elt that he wanted to see what their next move would be. Would Crum's men pack up and leave? Or would they continue to carry out Crum's plan?

Coladeus instructed Elt to lay low and await his next set of instructions. Coladeus figured that Crum wasn't about to give up, but he wanted to see what Crum and his men would do next. Elt concluded his conversation and headed back to Ralph's room.

In the days ahead, Elt knew communicating with the other neighborhood pets would be a challenge. School was out, so there would be no meetings at Juan's place, and if there was, Elt wouldn't be able to attend because Ralph was home. With Jenny staying with her grandparents some days, Elt wouldn't see Bernadette very much. Elt could meet her at night through the use of their doggie doors, but that was always a risk. Mr. Eltison, Ralph, Jenny, or Ms. Rodgers could wake up and discover their dogs missing.

When they did meet, the conversations were mainly about one topic; what were they going to do about the bad humans?

"Wait," replied Elt. "Coladeus will wait for their next move. We have to trust him. He and his crew have done so much for me . . . . for us."

"I hope he's right," said Bernadette. "I hate waiting around like this. I have a feeling that those bad humans are up to something, and it's no good."

Elt left that night with the same feeling that Bernadette was feeling. He wanted to do something. In the next few days, Elt would barely see his friend Bernadette, because Jenny stayed with her grandparents for a few days and there were no walks. Elt would have to continue the late night meetings with Bernadette and Jasmine in order to keep the communication flowing. That communication was very crucial, the fight against Crum and his men would take an even more evil turn in the coming weeks.

CHAPTER 12

"FOOLS! IDIOTS!" BLASTED CRUM AS he inspected the empty safe.

"But Mr. Crum, the safe was locked and the back door was shut," replied Frake. "All we did was go out and take care of more business. We didn't know."

Crum raised his hand. He had heard enough. He didn't want to hear excuses, although Frake was correct. Crum's men hadn't been careless; well maybe for leaving the back door open that one night, which led to the safe being broken into.

"Who do they think they are?" asked Crum to himself and his men around him. "I am the reason Bordertown exists, and I will own this town one day, too. Do they think they can do this and get away with it?"

Crum sat down at the table and rubbed his wrinkled hands together. Deep in thought, he started mumbling to himself.

"Does anyone have the foggiest idea of whom and what we're dealing with here?" asked Crum.

There was a moment of silence; then Frake raised his hand.

"Go on," uttered Crum.

"All we know is that they have a dog," replied Frake.

Crum sat silent for a few minutes, deep in thought. His men watched him, afraid to even blink an eye without the old man's permission.

"Well, first of all, whoever these fools are know our safe place," remarked Crum. "We'll have to find a new one. Take everything out immediately and rent this place out."

"And second, we need to find out who owns that dog," added Frake.

"And fourth, find out who is strong enough to open that safe," said Bull.

The men displayed a confused gaze at each other. Bull smiled, proud of his remark. Crum shook his head.

"You mean third, you idiot," blasted Crum.

Bull's smile disappeared.

Crum was one not to give up so easily. Although the money from the safe was missing, they still possessed their houses in Spring Valley and had started to rent those houses at very high prices. Crum still had plenty of money to replace what was lost, but he despised the thought of having to use his own money to carry out his plan. He was still determined to take over Spring Valley, and that one incident wasn't going to stop him.

The plan was set. After Crum returned to his car, driven by Sid, and left for Bordertown, Frake and his men began to move their operation. They located an old warehouse that had been deserted for quite some time on the outskirts of town. They purchased an old white van to help them move their furniture.

The warehouse, an old storage facility, was located on Observatory Road, which was about three miles past the Spring Valley Shopping Center near the town limits. The warehouse belonged to the Science and Observatory Lab, which was located a mile past the warehouse.

The warehouse used to store scientific equipment, files, and other materials needed for the observatory. As the years passed, the observatory constructed new buildings on its campus, so the extra space down the road wasn't needed anymore.

The observatory and all of its buildings were owned by Professor Eric Van Hausen. The professor and his associate scientists studied the stars and everything that was science related. He was fascinated with the subject of time travel, and had written several books on that subject. He had dabbled with the idea of trying to construct a time machine himself, but could never receive enough funding. Folks thought that although the idea was interesting, they felt that a time machine could never be built and a great deal of money would be wasted. So people basically left the professor alone. They figured whatever he was up to, as long as he didn't cause the town any trouble, he was okay. If the professor and his crew would have been more observant, they would have noticed an alien landing a pod ship within a few miles of the observatory.

When Frake approached the professor about renting out his warehouse space, Van Hausen was elated to receive some rent money for his vacant building. The lease papers were written in a day and the warehouse was rented.

Frake wasn't sure how long he and his men were going to reside at the warehouse, but it was far away from the old hideout. Whoever did break into their old storefront would be surprised to find an empty set of rooms the next time they showed up.

By the end of the week, the operation had been totally relocated to the new location on Observatory Road. Coladeus and his crew had been monitoring the old location at different times of the week, but never caught a glimpse of Crum's men moving their furniture. When they photographed images of the old hideout a couple of days later, Matheun noticed that the rooms were vacant and there was a FOR RENT sign on the front window.

The warehouse wasn't as accommodating as the first hideout. It was in pretty bad shape. The building was mainly metal, so it was very hot in the summer. The men constructed a living space where the office of the facility used to be. They laid down a piece of carpet, moved furniture and appliances into that space, and installed an air conditioner in one of the windows. Frake and his men also repaired the toilet and sink fixtures. They purchased a new safe since the old safe's door was broken.

Phase one of the operation was now complete. The men had successfully changed their hideouts without detection. Now came phase two. The plan was simple. Find the dog, and then find the owner who was responsible for returning all of their stolen goods. Little did these men know that the ones responsible for the dog and interference in their affairs were many miles away in deep space.

Frake's plan was to drive through every neighborhood in Spring Valley. They would not stop looking until they found the dog, maybe in a yard or walking in the streets. Frake vaguely recalled the family that Elt was with the day of the picnic. He remembered Elt, especially when the canine was in his hideout. He figured Elt was not a stray. Could the family he belonged to be responsible for the break-in of their old hideout?

Frake and his men started in the downtown area. They drove up and down First Street. They checked Main Street, Maple Avenue, and all the neighborhoods in that vicinity. There were plenty of dogs, but not the one they were searching for.

They checked the park on three different occasions. They saw all kinds of pooches. There were beagles, poodles, dachshunds, and German shepherds. No dog even came close to the wanted dog on their list.

On the fourth day, on an early summer evening in June, Frake, his brother, and Bull drove through the Valleydale subdivision. They hadn't traveled far before they found the dog they had been looking for.

On that day, Ralph had just finished dinner with his dad when he received a phone call from Jenny Rodgers. She hadn't seen Ralph for a few days and wondered if he would meet her and the dogs for a walk. Ralph helped his dad with the dishes, asked his dad, and after Mr. Eltison's approval, grabbed the leash and headed straight for Jenny's house with Elt.

The two kids and their dogs had just left Jenny's house and were walking on Valleydale Drive when a black sedan drove by. The car's windows were up because the air conditioning was on, plus Frake didn't want anyone to see his, his brother's, or Bull's faces. Elt was so elated that he and Bernadette were walking, that he never noticed the car drive by. He had only ever seen that car at night.

"I think we found our dog," said Frake calmly.

"But he's with a couple of kids and another mutt," added Jake.

"Let's drive around and see where they live," replied Frake.

The three men drove their vehicle around Springhaven Court and circled back to Valleydale Drive. They parked their vehicle near Mr. Davis's house where Sarge lived. After the kids and dogs walked for awhile, Ralph and Elt dropped Jenny and Bernadette at the Rodger's house and headed home. Frake, Jake, and Bull noticed where Jenny and Bernadette resided. They waited for Elt and Ralph to walk down Valleydale Drive and veer left on Springhaven. They followed the boy and his dog from a safe distance until Ralph and Elt entered their yard.

"See, it's just a kid and his dog," said Jake. "That kid can't pull a safe door open."

Frake remained silent as Ralph and Elt headed for the backyard.

"We'll come back later and check things out," said Frake.

As the black sedan drove by the Eltison house, Elt turned around as he walked with Ralph, and then he stopped. Elt sensed something different about the car; like he had heard that car drive by before, but not in that neighborhood. Elt couldn't see who was in the car, but then he realized it. He knew exactly who that car belonged to.

The bad humans weren't gone, and somehow they traced their way back to Elt. Maybe they were just checking out new neighborhoods to rob or steal from, but Elt didn't want to take any chances. Elt barked out a warning call to all the neighborhood animals about the intruders.

"What is it, boy?" asked a startled Ralph, who didn't understand why Elt was barking.

Ralph glanced back towards the road; he saw nothing. The black car had already passed. Hopefully one of the dogs or Jasmine heard Elt's warning. Elt followed Ralph inside, the sun was setting. It was going to be a long night.

Elt couldn't sleep that night. He walked around the house and kept a lookout for the black car. Elt circled the yard continuously, and then would do a sweep of the inside just in case. He was afraid to leave his yard and find the other dogs or Jasmine. Elt didn't want to leave his humans unprotected.

Elt yelped out another series of warning barks. No one responded. Where was everyone tonight? The bad guys may be there any minute and yet no one but Elt knew about it. Elt figured that all of his friends were asleep. Great. What a night for everyone to be asleep except for Elt. There was no sign of Jasmine, either.

During one of the times that Elt patrolled the inside of the house, the black car drove slowly down Springhaven Court, but the opposite way so that the car wouldn't drive by Ralph's house. Jake parked the car behind one of Mr. Dawkins's cars that he parked in front of his house. Jake turned off the engine and the lights.

Frake nabbed a set of binoculars and staked out Elt's house and yard. The view was pretty close with the help of the specs. Ten minutes later, Elt appeared into Frake's view.

Elt walked into the front yard. There was just enough light shining from both the moon and the street lamps for Frake to view Elt in his yard. Elt paced around the yard a few times. He was so anxious about the threat of Crum's men being around, Elt felt like he had to burn up some energy.

Elt began to dash quickly around the house. Not knowing he was being watched, Elt then jumped on and off the house several times.

"I don't believe what I'm seeing," remarked Frake.

Jake, who had began dozing for those ten minutes, opened his eyes and witnessed the same events.

"I don't need those specs to see what I'm seeing," said Jake. "That dog just jumped at least twelve, make it thirteen feet high."

Bull awoke from his slumber in the back seat of the car.

"Maybe it's not a real dog"' interjected Bull.

"You mean he's like a robot or something?" asked Jake.

Elt abruptly stopped jumping and stood still for a moment. He received a transmission from Coladeus. Elt immediately reported what he saw to his mentor. Elt was still not aware he was being watched.

"We've discovered that Crum's men have moved out of their old hiding place," reported Coladeus. "We have to be careful. These humans will stop at nothing to forge ahead with their plan. Please keep all of your friends aware."

Coladeus concluded his conversation with directions for their next strategic plan in dealing with Crum and his men. What was their plan? First, find the new hideout. Second, meet them face-to-face, and last, kick them out of Spring Valley for good!

"What's that dog doing?" asked Jake.

"Looks like he's talking or something," returned Frake as he continued to gaze through his binoculars.

"What?" asked Bull.

"I know it's hard to believe, but we just witnessed this dog jump on and off his roof," replied Frake.

"You mean to tell me that the dog is talking to himself?" inquired Jake.

"Sure looks like it's talking," said Bull, squinting to try and obtain a better view.

"You know, maybe we've been wrong the whole time about this dog," remarked Frake. "Maybe the dog is the one who opened the safe."

"You mean that dog has super strength?" asked Bull.

"Maybe he is a robot," added Jake.

"And maybe he's getting orders from someone else," added Frake. "I'd love to have that dog work of us."

"So how do we catch him?" asked Jake.

"I'd say we go find out more now," said Bull as he prepared to leave the back seat and confront Elt.

"No, wait!" said Frake. "He'll see us. We need to outsmart him and whoever he's working for."

"How do we do that?" asked Jake.

Frake scratched the hair on his chin and thought for a moment. Then he came up with an idea.

"We have to give him a reason to come after us without whoever he's working for knowing about it," said Frake. "I have the perfect plan."

Just as Elt walked back into the house, the car drove off, and headed back to the warehouse on Observatory Road. After a long night of guarding his property, Elt fell asleep in the kitchen as soon as he entered through his doggie door.

The next morning a white van pulled up in front of the Rodger's house on Valleydale Drive. It was a plain white van with a couple of ladders secured to the top. Three men stepped out, dressed in painter's cover-all uniforms, and grabbed a couple of paint cans and brushes.

They opened the front gate and entered the yard. These were no painters. The last man, which was Bull, grabbed a large net attached to a stick, similar to what a dog catcher would use.

Ms. Rodgers and Jenny had left earlier in the morning. Ms. Rodgers had to drop Jenny off with her grandparents. No one was in the house except for Bernadette.

Once inside the yard, the three "painters" pretended to set up shop. One placed the paint cans on the porch, while the other two set drop cloths on the ground. Frake wiped his brow with his sleeve. He checked the area for any nosy neighbors.

"Let's go to the back yard," said Frake as he walked toward the back of the house.

Jake and Bull picked up the supplies and followed Frake. All it took was a little banging on the back porch to send out a barking Bernadette out of her doggie door and into the yard. She saw Frake, but not Bull who was behind her. Bull easily snatched her with the net. Bernadette struggled, barked, and whimpered. No matter how hard she tried, she couldn't free herself.

"Mission accomplished!" exalted Bull as he hung a drop cloth over the net and carried Bernadette to the van. Frake led the way to make sure no one was looking while Jake followed with all of the supplies. Before she entered the van, Bernadette belted out one more yelp, hoping that Elt and her friends would hear that she was in trouble.

Before they drove away, Frake tore off a small piece of his clothing, wiped the cloth on Bernadette through the net holes, and laid the cloth on the ground in front of the fence.

Why did he do that? Simple . . . . to leave Elt a clue of Bernadette's whereabouts.

Jasmine heard the yelp all the way from her yard. She had been lying down on her front porch. She ran all the way to Valleydale Drive, but all she saw was a white van in the distance.

Elt was lying down on the kitchen floor, still exhausted from all of the work he had performed the night before. Even though hearing wasn't one of his super powers, Elt was a dog. He could easily hear his friend's yelp from a block away. Elt ran out of the kitchen through the doggie door and raced all the way to his fence.

Ralph had been sitting at the kitchen table, finishing his bowl of cereal. Ralph jumped off his chair, ran to nab his shoes, and followed Elt. Elt wanted to jump the fence and try to locate Bernadette, but he knew he couldn't at the time, he didn't want to show off any of his powers to Ralph.

Ralph caught up with Elt, who had his front two paws on the top of the fence.

"What is it boy?" asked Ralph.

Elt yelped out a series of cries and barks. Ralph looked down the street, but he saw nothing.

"There's nothing boy," said Ralph. "Maybe you just want to go for a walk."

Ralph ran back inside and fetched the leash. Elt usually never went for walks in the morning, but due to the circumstance involved, he didn't mind going out, because something was wrong with Bernadette.

Without using his new found talents, Elt had to stay in pace with Ralph, but he still practically dragged his human all the way to Jenny's house. Elt waited for Ralph to open the gate.

"Doesn't look like anyone's home boy," said Ralph.

Elt pushed forward and sniffed around for clues. He searched and sniffed the back door area, and picked up on both the stranger's and Bernadette's scents. Ralph called out for Bernadette about ten times, but she never came out of the doggie door.

Ralph and Elt moved back to the front yard. Elt sniffed around and ended back by the front gate. Once outside the gate, Ralph shut the gate while Elt discovered the piece of torn cloth that Frake had discarded intentionally. When Ralph turned away, Elt grabbed the cloth, and moved it to the curb. He would retrieve it later, for it was a definite clue.

Ralph and Elt walked all the way to Schoolhouse Road, but there was nothing. Elt knew what happened. Elt knew Bernadette was gone. She had been taken. He didn't know exactly why they took her, but they did.

It was all up to Elt to find her. Elt turned the other way. Ralph started to head back. It was evident that all Elt wanted to do was go home.

CHAPTER 13

LOST DOG WAS THE SIGN posted on almost every telephone pole in the Valleydale subdivision, as well as many adjoining neighborhood poles and lampposts. A picture of Bernadette along with the description of Jenny's Cocker Spaniel was listed on the poster, as well as all of the owner information. The signs were stapled and taped everywhere one day after Bernadette was discovered missing.

Wendy Rodgers had picked Jenny up from her grandparent's house and drove home. The front gate was latched. The front and back doors were locked. The only way Bernadette entered and exited the house was through the doggie door. There was no way, however, for her to escape.

Jenny was both sad and worried, but they waited the night just to make sure that Bernadette made it home.

Although Jenny was quite upset, she was determined to find her dog. She helped her mom create the lost dog signs, photocopied the signs, and posted them all over town. Ms. Rodgers took the day off from work to handle the family emergency.

Jenny and her mom had help, Jenny called Ralph that evening when she came home and discovered Bernadette missing. Ralph informed Jenny that Elt acted a little weird earlier that morning, and forced Ralph to check on Bernadette, but she wouldn't come out.

"Elt must have known something was wrong," concluded Ralph.

So Ralph, Jenny, and her mom started posting signs in their neighborhood. They moved downtown and posted signs. They also journeyed uptown.

Jenny continued to call Bernadette's name, hoping to hear some kind of a bark or see her loving dog race to her. Nothing happened. Holding back tears, Jenny forged on.

Ralph attempted to keep Jenny's mind off Bernadette that night, but it was a tough task. When Ralph went home with Elt, it was already dark. Ralph had called his dad earlier and asked to stay later than normal. Mr. Eltison knew where Ralph was and told Jenny's mom it was okay for Ralph to stay as long as he was helping her and Jenny.

Elt couldn't wait for Ralph to go to sleep that night, for he had plans of his own. His mind was set on rescuing Bernadette, but didn't realize what dangers lie ahead of him.

As soon as Ralph and his dad fell asleep, Elt set out to rescue Bernadette. He raced out of his doggie door and headed towards Bernadette's yard to retrieve the scrap of clothing he left near the curb in front of her house.

"Hey, where are you going?" asked Jasmine as she appeared out of the darkness.

Elt stopped for a moment.

"I have to keep going, I have to find Bernadette," returned Elt.

Jasmine jumped in front of Elt.

"I've tried to reach you all day, but you were gone," stated Jasmine.

"Yeah, my human and Bernadette's human were searching for her all day," said Elt. "I was with them. I think she was taken."

"I saw a big human transport machine take off in front of Bernadette's house yesterday morning," said Jasmine.

"I think it's those bad humans," returned Elt.

"You need some assistance?" asked the feline.

"Sure, but it may be a long way," answered Elt.

"As long as we make it back by morning," said Jasmine.

So the two set off for wherever Bernadette was in the middle of the night, not realizing what real danger they were in. Coladeus hadn't called the last two evenings, so he wasn't aware of what was going on with Elt or the missing Bernadette.

Elt stopped in front of Bernadette's house, found the torn piece of clothing, and gave it a good, long sniff.

"Pick up anything yet?" asked Jasmine.

"Yeah," Elt replied. "Let's go!"

Elt started off, but was way too fast for Jasmine, so the tabby climbed on Elt's back and went for a ride. What would have taken more than an hour took about fifteen minutes for the speedy Elt. He halted and took another sniff.

Elt and Jasmine scanned the area around them. They were on the outskirts of town, in an area where neither had been before.

"Are you sure we're headed in the right direction?" asked Jasmine.

"This way! Hold on!" Elt continued.

Elt blasted off again with the tabby on his back holding on. They soon stopped in an old graveled lot. Tucked in the back of the property was an old warehouse.

"The trail ends here," said Elt.

With the exception of an old street light on the opposite side of the property, the only other light was in the front window of the old warehouse.

"You think she's in there?" asked Jasmine.

"I don't know, but we need to be real careful just in case," answered Elt.

Elt and Jasmine crept to the back of the warehouse. They stopped at the rear door entrance. Elt checked the door to see if it was open. To his surprise, the door was slightly open. He slowly pushed the door. Jasmine jumped off Elt's back. They both entered slowly into a dark, vast room. All they could see were old crates lined up ten feet high on either side of them. At the end of the crate tunnel, there was a light in view.

"Stay here," Elt instructed Jasmine.

Jasmine nodded and remained in the shadows. Elt continued to walk towards the lighted area. He then started to hasten his walk when he saw what was under the hanging light. It was a cage, and in that cage was Bernadette. She had a muzzle on over her snout. She was trying to bark something to him, but the muzzle prevented him from understanding her. Bernadette was attempting to warn Elt.

"Bernadette! You're alive!" Elt barked. "Don't worry, I'll get you out!"

The cage was on the floor, surrounded by dozens of old crates. Bernadette kept trying to warn Elt, but all he heard were muzzled sounds. Elt attempted to break open the lock on the cage with his mouth.

All of a sudden, a giant nylon net was dropped on Elt. Frake jumped from behind a crate and tied one end of the net. Then another net fell, and then another. Bull and Jake leaped from behind more crates. The three men tightened and wrapped Elt to the point where he could hardly move. Even with his super strength, Elt was powerless, the more he tried to move, the more he got tangled, much like a spider's prey in a web.

Jasmine had slowly crept to where Elt was captured. She witnessed it all.

"It was a trap," Jasmine said to herself.

She scurried out from where she entered. Jasmine didn't stop until she jumped to the safety of her front porch, almost two hours later.

Elt had been captured. He had been out-smarted. Frake reached in and unfastened Elt's collar. Once the collar was removed from around Elt's neck, he felt his powers start to diminish. Frake inspected the collar. He noticed the small stone adhered to the back of the collar, but didn't know what it was.

"Don't see anything here," remarked Frake to himself as his cohorts continued to wrestle and constrict Elt.

"Looks like a little green stone on the bottom side of this collar," continued Frake to the others. "Weird how it's on the wrong side of the collar."

Luckily, the stone wasn't glowing; it was more of a dull lime green in color. Frake threw the collar down on the floor. That was a mistake, Frake didn't know what the stone on the collar was all about. Frake had witnessed Elt talking either into the collar or to himself, but he never made the connection between the collar and Elt's powers.

Frake and the boys weren't finished with Elt. He continued to wiggle and squirm, but he couldn't break free from the three layers of nylon nets. The next step for Frake was to move Elt into a cage, but in a way that he couldn't break out. Jake pulled out a pouch from his trouser pockets, and grabbed a handful of pellets in front of both Elt and Bernadette. The three men quickly applied gas masks over their faces. Smoke arose from the pellets and quickly sedated both Elt and Bernadette.

Bull dragged another cage across the floor. The men untangled a sleeping Elt from all of the nylon netting. They moved Elt into a new cage. They strapped his legs together so he couldn't move freely.

Morning came, and Ralph was presented with the same fate as his best friend. When Ralph awoke, Elt wasn't sleeping with him. Elt wasn't in the living room or the kitchen. Ralph checked all over the house. He went outside to scout the yard and dog house. The newspaper was still on the sidewalk. Elt always delivered the morning paper to his dad.

"Dad, have you seen Elt this morning?" asked Ralph.

"No Ralph, I thought he was with you," returned Ralph's dad, who was cooking some eggs and toast.

Ralph checked outside again while Ralph's dad walked into every room. There was no sign of Elt.

"I'm sure there is some reasonable explanation," said a calm Mr. Eltison.

"No Dad," Ralph returned. "Elt's gone to find Bernadette."

"Jenny's dog?" asked Mr. Eltison.

"Yeah," Ralph answered. "He was real upset yesterday when we couldn't find her. He wasn't himself."

So Ralph and his dad drove through the neighborhood. They both got out of the truck and walked for awhile. After two hours of searching, they drove home.

"We'll search some more in the afternoon," said Mr. Eltison. "I'm sure he's okay."

Ralph tried to hold back the tears. He was already upset about Jenny losing Bernadette. Now his dog was missing, too. What was going on?

Ralph's dad printed pictures of Elt off his computer, just like Jenny's mom had done the day before. They would post the pictures around town later that day, but Ralph hoped that Elt would find his way home before nightfall.

Ralph sat down on his back porch. He held Elt's leash in his hand. He stared at the dog house and ran his fingers through the braided fabric on the leash. Ralph had skipped breakfast, and ate very little for lunch. He had one thing on his mind . . . . to find Elt and Bernadette. Ralph glanced back at the doggie door.

"Stupid doggie door," said Ralph to himself. "I wish my dad never would have bought that thing."

Ralph's reasoning was that if the door wasn't there, Elt would have stayed inside and would have never left. The truth was that the doggie door had been very helpful. The doggie door's purpose was to give Elt the chance to go out if he needed to when there was no one else around.

Ralph thought long and hard for a moment. He knew that Elt was upset after Bernadette went missing. Ralph knew that if Elt did find her, they would head straight home.

Still, there was that uneasy feeling that something was wrong, especially with all the turbulence that Spring Valley had incurred that year. First, all of the robberies and mayhem were happening in the town. Money and valuables had been stolen. Then someone returned all the stolen merchandise. Now, pets were disappearing.

Would they return? Ralph had to remain positive. He hoped that the love for his dog and Jenny's love for Bernadette would help bring the dogs back safely.

For Jasmine, it had been a long, exhausting trek home from the warehouse. Panting heavily, the tabby collapsed on the front porch, and then gathered enough energy to drink the remaining water in her bowl. She watched the sky as dawn approached that morning.

Jasmine knew she had to recruit her friends to help rescue Elt and Bernadette, but it was going to be next to impossible. She possessed no super powers. She couldn't alert a human, there was no way she could convince one to follow her so far away.

Jasmine had to rest. Her eyes closed. She was happy she made it home. Jasmine knew she couldn't rest for long, but she was exhausted. When she woke, Jasmine knew she had a mission plan, a mission to save Elt and Bernadette.

CHAPTER 14

"WAKE UP!" A FAMILIAR VOICE exclaimed. "This is a matter of life and death!"

The animal behind the voice attempted to wake the sleeping beast. She nudged him with her head.

"I'm sleepy," the beast said with his eyes closed. "You're interrupting my nap time."

"I need your help!" the voice demanded. "Please! Get up now!"

The sleeping beast opened his eyes and found a feline nudging him with her head. It was Jasmine the tabby cat. Sarge yawned and stretched for a few seconds.

"Elt and Bernadette are in trouble and we have to help them!" Jasmine continued.

"What's all this about those two young whippersnappers being in trouble?" asked a groggy Sarge.

"The bad humans have Elt and Bernadette trapped in their new hideout," answered Jasmine. "We have to find a way to rescue them."

Sarge regained himself for a moment. He shook himself a couple of times and started pacing back and forth under his back porch. Jasmine explained the "up to the minute" news of why and how Elt and Berndatte wound up in an old warehouse. She told him about the new hideout and how Elt had been tricked and trapped.

"We need to hold an emergency meeting!" said Sarge.

Sarge continued pacing. Although he was rough and tough on the outside, he had a soft heart for Elt and Bernadette. He really liked those pups.

Jasmine raced over to Max's house. The Sheepdog was asleep, enjoying the coolness and comfort of the air conditioning. His aging body was a bit too old to handle the summer's relentless heat and humidity. Jasmine finally caught glimpse of Max when he went out later in the afternoon to take care of his business.

Jasmine then moved on to Juan's place. She peered into the window and searched for Juan. He too was inside napping. It would be an hour or so before she could get the Chihuahua's attention.

Lastly, Jasmine dashed over to Chin's dog house. He was inside meditating of course. The summer's sweltering heat was no deterrent for the Chow Chow. He remained calm and cool with his eyes closed.

By the time Jasmine reached all of the dogs, it was almost evening, so it was decided that they all meet at Juan's house when the sun was at its highest peak. It would be tricky, for Sarge, Max, and Chin would have to plan their "business" breaks before noon so they could get to the meeting on time.

After a very quick stop on her porch for a bite to eat and a drink of water, Jasmine raced back over to Sarge's dog house, where she and Sarge spent most of the night planning a rescue. These pets, who weren't used to that kind of pressure, had to devise a way not only to travel very far to reach their friends, but figure a way to outsmart those bad humans.

Just before Mr. Davis called Sarge into the house for the evening, the two hadn't really formulated anything positive. They still had no real ideas. All they did know was that they would have to work at night, while their humans were asleep. Each member of the team was going to have a specific job to do. They would have to work together as a team, there was no super strong dog to rely on.

For the last day and a half, Coladeus had tried to contact Elt, but he received no response. Elt and Bernadette were still asleep from the sleeping gas and the collar was still on the floor. It had been kicked by one of Frake's men in between a couple of boxes, so the men couldn't hear Coladeus's voice.

"Still getting no response," said Matheun.

"Do we have a location of the stone?" asked Coladeus.

"Yes, it is quite a distance away from where Elt has traveled previously," replied Mathuen. "But it has been in the same place for quite some time."

"I fear that something has indeed gone wrong," said Coladeus as he thought to himself.

"Should we set coordinates on the location?" asked Matheun.

"Have you been able to take any pictures?" asked Coladeus.

"Just the exterior," answered Matheun. "It seems to be some kind of metallic structure. We keep getting satellite interference from a set of structures close by."

Although Matheun didn't know what was causing the interference, the cause was the observatory, which housed buildings with very sophisticated equipment.

"Although I feel he may be in danger, I am still concerned about showing ourselves to humans," stated Coladeus. "Let's continue to monitor the situation a little while longer before we move in. I want to see if Elt and his band can do it on their own."

So the Trianthian ship waited, staying just far enough away from Earth's atmosphere so not to be detected. He didn't know the current situation, but as a Trianthian he had to be weary not to interfere locally, and especially risk the chance of being noticed. Having to deal with armies of humans because of visible exposure was something Coladeus wanted to avoid at all costs. He was counting on Elt and his friends to take care of the situation. He would wait a little longer.

Now that Elt and Bernadette were in cages, Frake and his boys weren't just going to sit around. With the super strong dog out of the way, they started back on their plan to overtake Spring Valley. Frake unrolled a long piece of paper and set it out on the table in their living quarters.

"It's time to hit hard and strike it rich early boys," said Frake.

The paper was a diagram of the Spring Valley National Bank. The diagram was labeled, from entrance to exit, guard positions, alarms, and most importantly, the safe.

"Instead of the middle of the day, we're gonna hit 'em in the morning, right when they open," explained Frake. "In fact, we should do it soon, like the day after tomorrow."

"But what if they're waiting for us since we've robbed them before?" asked Bull.

"They have most of their money back," said a familiar voice entering the room. "They think all the terrible things are over, but they will be surprised. I want my money back!"

From out of the warehouse and into the living quarters entered Crum, followed by his faithful henchman Sid.

"That's how we're gonna catch 'em off guard," added Frake. "In fact, we aim to take the whole safe this time . . . . rob the bank dry of all its money."

"Yeah, with that mutt in our hideout all tied up, we can do anything we want," triumphed Bull.

"But what about who's working with those dogs?" asked Jake. "We still don't know who we're dealing with."

"We'll have to be on our toes," said Frake. "We haven't seen these guys yet, we may never see them. Whoever they are, they're making their dog do all the work."

So the plan was set for Frake and his boys. They had met and planned their strategies. Whether they met the parties responsible for Elt and Bernadette didn't really much matter to them. They were moving forward with Elt under their control.

The next day, just before noon, the dogs and Jasmine gathered once gain in Juan's garage. Juan didn't set any biscuits out this time. Things were very serious.

"I'm afraid I can't walk that far," uttered Max. "These old legs just aren't up for it."

"That's okay Max," replied Jasmine. "We'll need someone here to keep an eye on things."

"Still that's going to be a long haul up to the new hideout," said Sarge. "I'm not sure if my legs can take it."

"We'll have to catch a ride on a human transport vehicle at least part of the way," explained Jasmine.

The pets all agreed with her suggestion. After about an hour of brainstorming, the pets finally devised some sort of a plan. They had no idea if it was going to work, but they were going to try and rescue their friends.

"Does everyone know where they're supposed to be?" asked Sarge as he paced back and forth in front of the group.

"Yes," answered Jasmine.

"Si," replied Juan. "I'm up in front."

"I'll be minding the fort," added Max.

Sarge lifted his paw in the air and motioned to Chin to make an announcement. What kind of proverb will he give them that day? Chin was in deep thought. He then lifted his head up to address his friends.

"You can't have bread without butter," said Chin.

Although it took a few moments to sink in, the pets realized what Chin was saying. It was once again a teamwork slogan. Chin was in. He wanted to be part of the team.

"So we meet here tonight after our humans go to sleep," stated Sarge.

"I believe I'm part of this neighborhood," echoed a voice just outside Juan's garage door.

A collective drop of cat and dog jaws would have best described the scene after the voice had spoken. In the doorway walked an ominous figure, much larger than Elt or any of the other dogs in the room. A figure in the past who had been quoted as saying he "was too good for the rest of the neighborhood" or that "he shouldn't be seen in the same yard with". The figure walked piously into the middle of the room.

It was Prince the Doberman, Mr. Dawkins's prized possession. An award winner in both local and regional dog shows for obedience and show, Prince was of only the finest grade. Prince gazed below at each of the pets and then finally stopped. He sat at attention in front of Sarge.

"I've heard what's been going on here," said Prince. "I feel that it is time for me to offer my professional assistance."

Sarge edged closer to Prince. He stared straight into the Doberman's eyes.

"We don't need your help," commanded Sarge. "We have it all under control."

Prince shoved his nose up in the air and stepped back a couple of steps. Jasmine jumped down from the rafters and stood next to Sarge.

"You know, having Prince's size and talents would greatly improve our chances, especially up against so many humans while there's so few of us," stated Jasmine.

Sarge thought for a moment. He knew Jasmine was right, but Prince had always thought pretty poorly of all the neighborhood dogs he lived near, and Sarge took those feelings to heart. He stared down at the floor.

"You figure out what to do with him," said Sarge reluctantly.

"We're all on the same team," said Jasmine. "We're here to save Elt and Bernadette. They helped save our town, our neighborhood. Now it's time to help them."

Sarge kicked his right paw a couple of times on the floor, and then turned his head slightly in Prince's direction.

"Welcome to the neighborhood," grumbled Sarge.

"Apology accepted," returned Prince calmly.

Sarge snarled, but Jasmine stepped in between the two dogs.

"Then it's done," declared the tabby. "We meet here tonight."

As the pets departed back to their homes, all that was left was for the humans to go to sleep. At the Eltison house, sleep had not been an easy task. Mr. Eltison was up late, making phone calls to friends and neighbors, and canvassing the different neighborhoods searching for two lost dogs. He hardly had enough time to finish his work.

Ralph didn't see Jenny much that day, for Jenny had to stay at her grandparent's house. Ms. Rodgers would continue her search for Bernadette when she returned home from work, but she had to report to work that day.

Ralph cried himself to sleep that night. He stared at the space Elt usually occupied every night when they went to bed. His dog had helped Ralph through so much. Now he was gone, nowhere in sight. What happened to Elt? And where was Bernadette? Were they alive? Were they safe? Things had been going so good, but now Ralph was sad again.

Ralph prayed that night for the two dogs. Little did he know that his prayers were being answered. An attempt was being made to save Elt and Bernadette.

CHAPTER 15

MRS. PEREZ ALWAYS RETIRED EARLY to bed at night, so it didn't take long for Juan to escape through his doggie door and out to the garage. He had to prepare the garage for their meeting and then departure.

There was never a problem for Jasmine to sneak out in the evenings. She was primarily an outdoor cat anyway, except for some of those really cold evenings. Mrs. Reed would find her a cozy spot by the fireplace. Soon Jasmine was waiting alongside Juan for the others to arrive.

The challenges for the trip were going to be Max, Prince, Sarge, and Chin. Each dog usually spent their nights indoors with their humans. Another disadvantage for them was that they didn't own doggie doors, so they would have to be creative in their escape attempts.

Max slipped a small toy left by one of Mrs. Petrie's grandchildren in between the back door and the threshold. When Mrs. Petrie shut the door at night, she didn't realize that the door didn't fully engage. Max grabbed his old leash and fit the handle around the doorknob. After a couple of tugs, the back door was open. It wasn't long before Max finagled the gate latch open and arrived at Juan's garage. Max's only challenge left was to stay awake; a dog of his age was not used to "all nighters" without a nap. He had to remain ready and awake, even if he was staying there and making sure things were calm at headquarters.

Sometimes Mr. Davis would allow Sarge to stay out all night if his dog insisted on staying out, but he preferred to have his pet inside for the night. That night Sarge had "put on a real show", and it worked. While inside, Sarge kept barking and scratching at the door until Mr. Davis let him out.

"If you're going out, then you'll be staying out for the night Mister," said Mr. Davis to his Boxer. "Don't expect me to wake up in the middle of the night to let you in."

That was exactly what Sarge had planned. He didn't want his human searching for him in the middle of the night, especially if he was far away.

Chin just used stubbornness as his excuse to stay out that evening. When it was time for him to walk inside, Chin just sat at attention by his doghouse. Mrs. Yao pleaded with him, but he wouldn't budge. Finally, she just shrugged her shoulders and gave up. She closed the door and turned off the back light. He was free to trek over to Juan's house.

Now Prince tried the same tactic, but Mr. Dawkins would have nothing to do with it. He walked his prized possession inside. Prince had to create a new plan and fast. He remembered something about Mr. Dawkins that might save him.

Mr. Dawkins did have one bad habit. On many nights, Mr. Dawkins would fall asleep without shutting the back door, leaving only the screen door shut. Feeling unsafe about leaving the back door open wasn't really a concern, for in his house lived an alert Doberman.

Once he escorted Prince inside, Mr. Dawkins forgot to shut the back door, and fell asleep on his recliner watching television. That was the break Prince needed, as soon as his human fell into a deep slumber, Prince easily pushed himself out the screen door and nudged his gate open. Prince was the last to arrive at Juan's garage.

"What took you so long?" asked Sarge to Prince as he entered the garage. "We almost left without you."

"I was waiting for my human to retire for the evening," replied Prince.

"We have no time for this," said Max. "You all have to go now! It will be difficult for you to make it back before morning, but you will have to do your best."

"That's the chance we'll have to take," said a determined Jasmine.

So the pets raced off, following Jasmine's trail. Leading the way, Juan and Jasmine had to stop every once in a while to allow the larger dogs to catch up with them.

Although it was very late, and there were only a few cars out on the road, there was still going to be a challenge for the pets to stay hidden. They did have a long way to travel. The pets would have to stay low, especially out of their neighborhood, for if one human witnessed all of the pets together, chances of them getting away and rescuing their friends would be slim.

When the group reached Pleasant Grove Road and had already turned left towards the warehouse, Jasmine noticed a flatbed truck stopped at a traffic light.

"Do you think he's heading where we need to go?" asked Jasmine.

"He's going our way," said an already weary Sarge. "Here's our chance."

Just before the traffic light turned green, the pets jumped up onto the flatbed truck and hid beneath a tarp that was covering the driver's load. The driver never heard a thing, for he had his radio on kind of loud.

After about a mile and a half up the road, the driver put on his right turn signal and started to turn. The pets could all feel the truck turning, so they decided to jump. One by one, starting with Juan, the pets leaped down onto the side of the road. The flatbed driver gazed up at his rear view mirror. He thought he saw something move, but when he glanced again, he saw nothing. All of the dogs plus Jasmine had jumped to safety. Lumped together like a clump of grapes, the pets hid in the tall grass along the side of the road.

Jasmine and the group still had a ways to go, but the trip on the flatbed saved some valuable time. Jasmine jumped onto Prince's back for the rest of the trip. Sarge and Chin were tired, but kept up the pace as they were nearing the warehouse.

By the time they reached their destination, daybreak was fastly approaching. The trip had been very taxing on all of them. Sarge and Chin were panting for water. Juan was still vibrant and hyper as ever.

Prince remained calm. If he was tired, he didn't show it. Jasmine was exhausted, but carried on. This was the second extensive trip she had taken in two days.

"We need to find water before we move on," demanded Sarge. "I need to regain my strength."

"Elt and Bernadette are just up ahead," said Jasmine. "We can make it."

"I could use a little refreshment," said Prince.

"Wilted flower needs water too," added Chin.

There hadn't been any rain lately, so there were no visible water puddles to drink from. Jasmine and the others searched around as they saw the warehouse straight ahead.

"Look, that is the place up ahead," said Jasmine. "Maybe there's some water there where the bad humans are. We have to keep moving before it gets any lighter."

Jasmine was right. They were already going to be missed by their humans, so rushing back was pointless. They were at the site, so they had to give their rescue plan a chance. Elt and Bernadette needed their help.

Juan was the first one to locate water. In the back of the warehouse, near an old gas pump, were a couple of buckets of fresh water that Frake and his men must have used and left out. Each dog and Jasmine took their turns, two at a time, to refresh themselves. Once they finished, the dogs and Jasmine ran over to the back of the building near the back door.

"Let's see if it is unlocked," said Sarge.

"Maybe they were lazy and left it open," added Juan.

"Be careful," said Jasmine. "The last time it was open, it was a trap."

Prince walked up to the door. Since he was by far the tallest, Prince could reach the doorknob easiest. He tried nudging the door, but it was locked. He turned around to give the "no" nod of his head to the others, but then was suddenly alerted. Someone was coming.

"Humans are coming!" said Prince in a low voice.

Prince darted away from the door. He and the others ran to the side of the building away from where Crum's and Frake's vehicles were. They all peeked out from the corner to get a view of who was coming out.

The door opened. Out came Frake, Bull, Jake, and Jeb.

"You know the plan, right?" asked Frake to his cohorts.

The men groaned and nodded in agreement. They walked over to the black sedan.

"First we get some breakfast, and then we're off to finish the job," continued Frake.

Jake started the car and they drove off.

Once they left, Juan sped over to the door and then ran back.

"We're in luck," said Juan. "The door is open a little."

Juan was correct. The last human to leave, Jeb, didn't shut the door properly. The pets ran over to the door. Jasmine jumped on top of Prince again. She stood up and pushed the door open with her paws. The door opened enough for all of them to fit through.

Once inside, the group slowly passed by rows and rows of boxes. Jasmine knew her way, so she led her friends to where Elt and Bernadette were the last time she saw them. She glanced upward a couple of times, making sure that no human was above with nets. Jasmine didn't want to fall into the same trap Elt had fallen into.

Bernadette, who no longer was muzzled, was lying down. Bull had removed it while she was asleep. She hadn't made a sound, so he kept it off of her. Elt was still groggy from all the sleeping gas he inhaled. He was barely awake when he thought he saw something, but figured it was a dream. Elt saw his friends, and even Prince, in front of him.

Elt opened his eyes. It wasn't a dream! In front of him, he saw his friends coming towards him. Bernadette saw them, too.

"How did you?" she asked.

"Stay quiet," said Jasmine as she searched around for any sign of danger. "Are there any more humans?"

"Two up in that room," answered Bernadette.

Bernadette was referring to the living quarters at the front of the warehouse. Sarge and Prince attempted to open Elt's cage, but it was secured with a giant padlock. Chin tried to open Bernadette's cage, but she had a lock on the cage, too.

"How are we going to do this?" asked Sarge.

"I have an idea," replied Elt. "Juan, under that box, fetch me that collar please."

Prince nudged the box upward. Juan retrieved the collar and ran over to the cage.

"Now, see if you can squeeze the collar inside the cage to me," instructed Elt.

Juan, with Jasmine's assistance, slid the collar through the holes of the cage. Elt picked up the collar with his mouth and swung it around his neck. Then he moved closer and pinned himself against the cage. Both Juan and Jasmine slipped their paws inside the cage holes and finagled the collar straps around Elt's neck. Within a minute or two, Juan and Jasmine had successfully strapped Elt's collar. Hopefully, Elt would regain his strength faster than when he originally was introduced to the Trianthian stone. He tore away at the remaining straps that were constraining him.

Now Elt felt re-energized, so he attempted to pry open the door from the cage. The door still was chained with a lock.

"Stand back everyone!" Elt announced to all of his friends.

With all of his might, Elt applied pressure to the cage and tried to tear a whole wide enough with his paws. Nothing happened. After several failed attempts, Elt sighed and sat down for a moment.

"The stone must have been off me for too long," said Elt. "But we can't wait all day either for me to get stronger."

"You mean you're not that strong and fast now?" asked Juan.

"It's the stone on the collar," answered Elt. "Its energy gives me my powers."

All of a sudden, a welcomed voice was heard. It was Coladeus, trying once again to communicate with Elt.

"Elt, Elt, can you hear me?" asked Coladeus.

"Loud and clear," answered Elt. "But I need your help. My collar has been off for a long time. I've seemed to have lost a great deal of my strength."

Coladeus paused for a moment. All of the dogs watched Elt with amazement. Someone was really talking to Elt from somewhere; maybe it was really out of space.

"You are fine. You never lost your powers," said Coladeus.

"What do you mean?" asked Elt. "I just tried to bust down a door off this cage, and I failed."

"You had the collar on long enough to sustain your powers," returned Coladeus. "But in your mind, because the collar was off, you thought you've lost them. Try that cage again."

Everyone watched Elt once again. He took a deep breath, closed his eyes, and pushed on the cage door with all of his might. The chain holding the cage door snapped. Elt then easily pushed open the door with his front paws. Prince's jaw dropped as he couldn't believe what he had just witnessed.

Elt walked over to Bernadette's cage. He bit into the cage lock. It easily snapped in two. Elt opened the cage door.

"Simply magnificent! Amazing!" declared Prince.

"You see Elt, to be a superhero, or in your case, a super dog, one must always think he or she is super," stated Coladeus. "That stone has given you so much power, it would take a much longer absence away from it in order for you to lose it."

"Very wise words," Chin said softly.

Once Bernadette escaped out of her cage, the pets exchanged pleasantries briefly, so excited to see each other again. In his excitement, Juan accidentally let out a louder than normal yelp for a dog his size, then covered his mouth with his paw.

A few seconds later, a half-groggy Sid opened up his door and gazed out. He couldn't believe what he saw. A bunch of dogs and one cat running around in the warehouse! And Elt and Bernadette were out of their cages!

"What is this?" Sid shouted. "How did all of these animals get in here?"

For a few seconds, the dogs stood silent. Then Prince walked in front of Elt.

"Let me take care of this," said Prince.

Prince walked over in Sid's direction, picked up the pace almost to a trot, and wailed out the most horrific snarl and growl ever heard. The noise was so frightening that it would have made the hairs on anyone's arms stay straight at attention.

"Nice boy," trembled Sid as he backed up and began to shut his door.

At that point, a half-sleepy Walter Eugene Crum walked right into Sid as he was backing up.

"What the devil is going on out here?" inquired Crum.

"Back up Mr. Crum," said Sid. "We have company."

Sid shut the door. Elt walked up to Prince.

"Great work!" shouted Elt.

"I've still got it," answered Prince as he walked in a small circle around the pets.

Coladeus contacted Elt again on the transmitter.

"Elt, you now need to leave the bad human hideout," instructed Coladeus. "There is still work to be done."

"More work to be done?" questioned Sarge. "By golly, we just rescued these two pups. You mean there's more?"

"Affirmative," replied Coladeus. "Those humans are about to embark on another destructive mission. They are en route back to downtown Spring Valley. The bank may be their next target."

"We're on it," said Elt. "Come on, let's go!"

After a bit of grumbling from the larger dogs, the pets started back towards downtown Spring Valley. There was hope that some of them could catch a ride again from a flatbed or pick-up truck. Elt was ready to race toward the destination, but he wanted to keep an eye on his friends. After all, if it wasn't for his friends, Elt may have never escaped. He was lucky and grateful to have such really wonderful friends.

Once the pets left the warehouse, Crum and Sid slowly opened their door. Sid peeked out and saw no one.

"The coast is clear," said Sid.

Crum and Sid slowly wandered out of the living quarters and walked over to the cages. Sid noticed the door off its hinges on Elt's cage.

"Look boss, that dog must have gotten his strength back," said Sid.

Crum bent down to inspect the damages.

"We must move so we can pick up the boys after their mission," shrieked Crum.

"I'll get the car running," said Sid as he made his way to the back door.

Crum raised one of his hands.

"No need for that," said Crum. "I've arranged for some alternate transportation. Let's grab our things."

Crum and Sid walked back to the living quarters and shut the door behind them.

CHAPTER 16

"JUAN! JUAN! COME HERE JUAN! Where are you?" shouted Mrs. Perez.

She was deeply concerned. Her little Juan had never wandered away. When she awoke that morning, there were no signs of her Juan. She combed the inside and outside.

Mrs. Perez was not the only pet owner in the Valleydale subdivision that was concerned. Mr. Davis was also outside, searching for his Sarge.

"I just don't get it," said Mr. Davis. "Sarge has never run off like that."

"If your Sarge is missing, that makes four dogs this week missing," said Mrs. Perez. "The little Rodger's girl doggie and the little boy's dog on Springhaven Court.

"Prince never leaves the yard without me" boasted Mr. Dawkins.

"Something is definitely wrong," added Mrs.Yao. "Neither does my Chin."

When Mr. Eltison wheeled his garbage can out to the road that morning, he noticed all of his neighbors searching for their lost pets. The only relieved owner was Mrs. Petrie. After calling for her Max, the Sheepdog appeared from the back of Juan's house and slowly walked back to his yard. Max had remained at his post, awaiting the return of the rescue squad. Once he heard his human calling his name, Max realized that sooner or later he would be found, so he walked out of Juan's garage. Mrs. Petrie was grateful to see her Max, but was worried about the other dogs and their owners.

"Something is going on here!" declared Mr. Dawkins. "I think our dogs have been dog-napped."

"Plus Jasmine," added Mrs. Reed. "She's missing, too."

Sheriff Thomas responded promptly to the call. He heard all of the neighbors's stories about their missing pets, including Mr. Eltison, who never initially called the police but told his story, too.

All Sheriff Thomas could do was scratch his head. How could all of these dogs and one cat disappear?

"Were there any other reports of missing pets in Spring Valley?" questioned Mrs. Yao.

The sheriff just shook his head.

"No ma'am, this is the first time I received a report like this," said the sheriff. "But we'll keep an eye out for them."

Sheriff Thomas returned to his car and drove off. He circled the neighborhood a couple of times just in case he spotted any sign of the missing pets. He really should have been downtown, where another bank robbery was about to take place, but he didn't know.

"What do we do now?" asked Mrs. Reed.

"I'd say we go out looking for them," declared Mr. Davis.

"Grand idea!" exclaimed Mr. Dawkins. "I know my poor boy Prince is in trouble."

By that time, Ralph had walked outside to investigate all of the commotion. Ralph's dad was still talking to the neighbors.

"Dad, can we go too?" asked Ralph.

"Son, we spent the last day and a half looking," explained Ralph's dad. "We have posters everywhere and I've already taken a few days off work searching for both Elt and Bernadette.

"Can't we just go out for a little while?" Ralph asked.

"Just for a little while," said Mr. Eltison. "But we've got to get back so I can finish my work."

Ralph and his dad walked over to their truck and drove off. The group of neighbors, headed by Mr. Davis, headed for their vehicles.

Mrs. Petrie agreed to watch out for the pets while the others were away.

"We'll head into town," said Mr. Davis. "Maybe someone has seen them."

While the Valleydale neighbors searched for their pets, Elt and his group were traveling down Pleasant Grove Road as fast as they could, as a group that is. They realized that their humans had more than likely found them missing already, so going home now without trying to stop Crum's men would have been a bad idea. Elt was running too fast for everyone, and had to slow down to let the others catch up.

"You go ahead, we'll catch up to ya," said Sarge.

"No, we're a team," said Elt. "We'll go as a team."

Sarge admired Elt for that comment, and they forged on. Luck was on their side, for another flatbed truck stopped at the traffic light where the Spring Valley Shopping Center was located. All of the pets jumped aboard and hid themselves up against the cab of the truck.

The truck driver thought he saw something flash by, but through his rear view mirror he saw nothing. When he turned around, he caught a glimpse of a fluffy tuft of orange, for Chin's tail wagged back and forth.

The driver shook his head and continued driving. At the next stoplight, the driver turned around again, and Prince was staring at him through the window. The driver shook his head and continued driving when the light turned green.

"I need another cup of coffee," the driver said to himself.

By the time he was downtown and turned onto First Street from Main Street, the driver gazed back one more time. He saw no one. If there were dogs on his truck, they were gone. Once Elt noticed the bank, he knew it was time to jump, so when the driver slowed down to turn, they all leaped off the truck.

As the pets approached the bank, they noticed Mrs. Simon, the bank manager. She opened the front door and ushered in folks who were waiting to enter the bank. The pets ran into a back alley. Elt recognized the familiar black car parked in the back. Elt and the group hid behind a dumpster, not to be noticed by Frake, his men, or any humans.

A few minutes later, Frake and his men got out of the car.

"Me and Jake will take the front, Jeb and Bull take the back entrance," directed Frake.

The men chuckled as they slid their masks on. They figured the job would be easier, for no one was expecting a robbery that day. They also thought that the one dog that could stop them was locked up in their warehouse many miles up the road.

"Any sign of the cops?" asked Jake.

Frake looked around.

"Nothing," returned Frake. "Let's go."

The four men walked into the bank simultaneously, two through the front, and two back. They didn't realize they were being watched.

"There they are," said Elt.

"It's time to rock," declared Prince

"Yeah, I haven't bitten a butt since the mailman got too close to me a long time ago," added Sarge.

The dogs plus Jasmine ran straight for the back entrance of the bank. Mr. Drexel, who had walked over to the bank to deliver his deposits from the day before, caught a glimpse of Elt and a bunch of other dogs plus a cat, running across the alley. He remembered Elt's picture posted on one of the lampposts on Main Street. He reached into his pocket and grabbed his phone. He pulled out a piece of paper from his pocket. Mr. Drexel had been particularly concerned about Elt's disappearance, as well as Bernadette's, for he had both of those dogs in his pet store before.

"Hello Mr. Eltison, Drexel here," said the pet store owner. "This is going to sound weird, but I just saw . . . . well I think I saw your dog by the Spring Valley National Bank."

Mr. Drexel waited for Mr. Eltison's response.

"There's one more thing," continued Mr. Drexel. "He's running with a bunch of other dogs and one cat."

Back in Mr. Eltison's truck, Ralph's dad had just turned right onto Schoolhouse Road when he received the call from Mr. Drexel.

"Mr. Drexel just spotted Elt and the other pets," said Ralph's dad. "We need to alert the rest of the neighbors."

Mr. Eltison quickly stopped at the school parking lot so he could call Mr. Davis and Mrs. Reed, for Mr. Dawkins was riding with Mr. Davis and both Mrs. Perez and Mrs. Yao were riding with Mrs. Reed. He also phoned Wendy Rodgers. She was downtown working, just a few hundred yards away, so she might have been able to reach the pets first.

As soon as Frake and his men entered the bank from both the front and the rear with their disguises, they immediately went to work.

"Okay folks, this is a stick-up!" shouted Jake as he and Frake went up to Mrs. Simon, who was still walking around in the main lobby. The security guard lifted his hands in the air.

Bull and Jeb headed straight for the tellers. The customers were both scared and confused. How could there be another bank robbery?

Within seconds, Mrs. Simon was escorting Frake and his brother into the vault. The two men began dumping stacks of cash into very large bags. Bull and Jeb were filling all the teller drawers with money. It was too easy, so they thought.

The pets stopped in front of the back door entrance.

"Let me open it," said Prince. "I can open any door."

"No please, let me," asserted Elt. Elt gripped and pulled. He tugged so hard that the steel-framed door was torn from its hinges. Elt pushed the door to the side and braced it up against the back wall of the bank.

"Not the way I had planned to open it, but that will do," said Prince.

"Let's go!" yelled Bernadette.

What happened next not only boggled the minds of the citizens and tellers, but the bank robbers, too. Everyone, including Frake, Jake, Jeb, and Bull, froze in their skins when they heard the clamor of dog barking and one cat screeching originating from the back entrance.

The pets knew their roles, they planned out their strategy while catching the ride on the flatbed truck. Sarge and Chin lunged after Bull. Chin leaped at Bull's head, while Sarge aimed for the robber's butt. Crunch!!! Juan and Bernadette headed straight for Jeb. The spaniel tugged at Jeb's britches while Juan leaped onto his head. Jasmine assisted her friends by scratching and clawing at Jeb's hands. In a matter of seconds, both men were on the floor shielding themselves from the claws, bites, and scratches.

Jake walked out of the vault to find out what all the commotion was about. Jake was immediately confronted by Prince, who promptly knocked the human down. Prince just stood on him and growled, not allowing Jake to move.

"Nice doggie," uttered Jake nervously. "Uh Frake, a little help here."

Frake's fate was no different, for he had to face Elt the super dog.

"Oh no," said Frake. "He must have a brother."

Elt leaped onto Frake. The next thing folks witnessed was Frake being tossed around like a stuffed doll. Elt had a score to settle with Frake, especially with what had just happened in the warehouse.

Still in shock at what she had just witnessed, Mrs. Simon regained herself and threw open the front doors. Instead of folks coming in to make deposits at that moment, the bank made a deposit of its own. The four henchmen were dragged and then thrown onto the sidewalk. Sheriff Thomas was driving by when he noticed the men being kicked out of the bank. The sheriff stopped his car and threw open the door. Deputy Taylor threw open the station doors and ran across the street.

"Mrs. Simon, what the devil is going on here?" asked Sheriff Thomas.

"We were being robbed by these four terrible men, and these wonderful animals saved us!" declared a jubilant Mrs. Simon.

"Pets?" asked Sheriff Thomas.

Deputy Taylor secured handcuffs on two of the men and had to borrow more pairs from the sheriff. It was a wonder they had that many at all, for they had never had to use them before.

Lined up along the front wall of the bank were six dogs and a cat. Some of them panted heavily, for the morning's ordeal had been very tiring. Sheriff Thomas removed his glasses and stared at the pets.

"Well I'll be," Sheriff Thomas declared. "These animals stopped the robbery?"

"It's like they knew what they were doing," replied Mrs. Simon.

The sheriff examined the dogs and cat a little closer.

"You know, I think these are the pets that are missing from Valleydale," said the sheriff. "They must have been pet-napped by these men or something."

"Who would do such a thing?" asked Mrs. Simon.

"I'll tell you who," answered Deputy Taylor as he removed the masks off the four men.

By now, a huge crowd had gathered, including Mayor Helms, in front of the bank. There hadn't been so much commotion since the day Elt, Bernadette, and Jasmine returned all the money in front of the police station.

"Why it's those nice men who lived next door," announced Mrs. Simon as the rest of Spring Valley discovered the identity of the bank robbers. "Shame on you! How could you do such a thing?"

Frake barely lifted his head. All he could do was utter "Where's Mr. Crum?" before he threw his head down on top of Jake, who was leaning up against him.

"Sometimes that's how it goes," mentioned Sheriff Thomas. "The ones you think you can trust, you can't. I think Spring Valley has learned a valuable lesson today."

Ralph's dad pulled his truck into the bank parking lot. Wendy Rodgers was running up to the crowd when she spotted her daughter's Bernadette on the front steps of the bank. Shortly after, Mr. Davis's car and Mrs. Reed's van drove into the parking lot as well.

As Ralph and his dad exited their truck, they both noticed the crowd in front of the bank.

"What's going on out there?" asked Mr. Eltison.

Ralph and his dad sifted through the crowd to get a better view of what was going on. All they could see was four men in handcuffs surrounded by the deputy and the sheriff.

"Trying to rob the bank, they were," said one citizen to Ralph's dad. "Bunch of dogs got 'em I hear."

Ralph peeked and noticed Frake's face.

"Hey dad, that was the strange man at the park," said Ralph. "I knew he was up to no good."

The crowd's attention to the four men suddenly shifted to the sky above. Flying low enough to be recognized was Crum, Sid, and the helicopter pilot.

"Mr. Crum, help us!" yelled Frake.

Elt had never seen a flying machine like that before and it didn't resemble Coladeus's pod ship at all. He wanted to test the whole flying concept that Coladeus said might happen one day, but not in front of all of these humans.

Inside the copter, Crum knew that there was nothing he could do. His four men, including his most valuable asset Frake, had been captured by the authorities.

"Turn around, let's go," said Crum to the pilot in disgust.

"But Mr. Crum, we can't just leave our guys," said Sid.

"There will be a better time to get them out, but not now," returned Crum.

From below, Mrs. Simon noticed one of the three men that were seated in the helicopter.

"That's Mr. Crum!" shouted Mrs. Simon. "He was in this caper, too?"

Crum grabbed a microphone from the pilot.

"I'm not through with you citizens of Spring Valley!" blasted Crum. "I shall return! Walter Eugene Crum never loses!"

With those words, the helicopter flew off. Ralph stared at the copter as it flew away.

"Wow," said Ralph. "Just like Dr. Plasmo!"

The excitement and action continued, for now it was time for the pet owners of these heroic animals to come face-to-face with their amazing pets. Several citizens assisted the sheriff and the deputy in making sure that Crum's four men were escorted to the police department's jail.

"Really can't hold them for questioning," said Sheriff Thomas to Mrs. Simon as he walked off with the prisoners. He was referring to the dogs and cat that were still sitting in front of the bank entrance. "Folks that are here for your pets can take them home," the sheriff continued before he left.

Wendy Rodgers was the first one to retrieve her dog. Just as she walked up to the bank's front steps, Jenny came running up to the crowd yelling Bernadette's name. When Mr. Eltison called Wendy Rodgers a few moments earlier, Wendy notified her parents so that Jenny could meet her. Bernadette ran down the steps and lunged into Jenny's arms. Bernadette filled Jenny's cheeks with multitudes of sloppy dog kisses. Jenny was so excited to see her dog again.

Next, Juan darted down and found his human, Mrs. Perez. He leaped into her arms. Even though he was very small, so was Mrs. Perez, so Juan almost knocked her over. Of course Juan was excited to say the least.

Chin slowly walked down the steps and located his human, Mrs. Yao. She bent down and gave her orange, loveable dog a hug. His fluffy tail wagged constantly. Mrs. Yao and Mrs. Perez walked their pets over to Mrs. Reed's van.

Mrs. Reed called for her Jasmine. The feline wove her way through the crowd and found her human. Mrs. Reed had knelt down and waited for her cat to approach her. Jasmine rubbed her head up against her human. The feline purred and meowed as Mrs. Reed picked up her cat. The three ladies and their pets traveled home as soon as Mrs. Reed and Jasmine entered the van.

"Sarge!" yelled Mr. Davis. "Where are you boy?"

The Boxer eagerly ran and placed his front paws on his human. He barked a couple of times with joy.

"Hey Mister," said a boy standing in the crowd. "Your dog is a hero. He helped catch those bad guys."

Mr. Davis proudly hugged his dog.

"He's always been a brave dog, the best in the world!" exclaimed an elated Mr. Davis.

Mr. Davis reached into his pocket and presented his pet with a couple of dog biscuits. Sarge barely allowed Mr. Davis enough time to pull the treats out. Sarge nabbed the biscuits, for the leader of the Valleydale neighborhood pets was famished.

"Prince! Prince!" shouted Mr. Dawkins.

Prince majestically waltzed down the steps and then sat in front of his human without command. He valiantly raised his right paw for his human to shake. Mr. Dawkins shook his paw, and then hugged his courageous canine.

Jenny, Wendy, and Bernadette pushed their way through the crowd and found Ralph and his dad. After watching all the neighbors welcome back their pets, Ralph and his dad searched and located their dog.

"Only one more dog left!" announced Mayor Helms. "Who does he belong to?"

"Me!" screamed Ralph as he approached the bank's front steps.

"Elt!" exclaimed Ralph. "Oh Elt, come here boy!"

Elt, not trying to show off any super speed or leaping ability, ran slowly to meet his favorite human. He did almost knock Ralph over. Like his friend Bernadette, Elt licked Ralph's face continuously. A smiling Mr. Eltison bent down to pet Elt.

"Oh Elt, I thought I'd never see you again," said Ralph.

Jenny and Bernadette met Ralph and Elt with hugs and pet kisses. Wendy Rodgers watched and smiled to see her Jenny so happy that her pup was back. As they made their way to their vehicles, Jenny and Ralph agreed to take a break for the day with no walk, but they could resume the walks the next day when Jenny came home.

The rest of the day Ralph never once let Elt out of his sight. He knew that his dog was safe, but he had missed Elt so much, he wanted to spend the entire day with him.

It was a joyous moment for the citizens of Spring Valley. The bank robbery had been thwarted, the bad humans who had been causing all the trouble in the town were captured, and a neighborhood's lost pets had been returned safely to their homes.

Mayor Helms had declared that the six dogs and one cat were heroes. They were going to be honored in a grand ceremony during the town's Fourth of July celebration.

Although no words were exchanged between them after they were reunited with their owners, the dogs and cat from the Valleydale subdivision were at peace with themselves and each other. Elt was very grateful that his friends had rescued him and Bernadette. They had all worked together; old and young, big and small, dog and cat, to stop Frake and his men.

They would all meet again soon for their next pet meeting. Now that Spring Valley was safe again, there would be less talk and more doggie biscuits for Sarge to eat when they would meet in Juan's garage.

Elt was asleep with Ralph on the edge of Ralph's bed when he heard Coladeus calling him on the transmitter. Elt quickly rose and ran outside through the doggie door to the backyard. Elt filled Coladeus in with all the details about the dog-napping, the rescue, and the capture of the bad humans. Coladeus wasn't able to watch the events, for they had to leave Earth's atmosphere for a short time. Coladeus congratulated Elt on a job well done. He also wanted to pass along a very big thank you to all of Elt's friends.

"I have to leave soon, we have other civilizations that need our help," stated Coladeus. "But I will have new assignments for you and possibly your friends. Some of the assignments will be here on Earth, some may be very far away. You will continue to use your powers when needed, even if I'm not around, if you see fit of course. I trust that you will be wise in your decisions."

Before the Trianthian leader signed off, he informed Elt that he would visit him the next evening before leaving Earth.

"Please be prepared for my arrival," Coladeus instructed before he signed off.

Elt had completed his first assignment. He and his friends had fought a tough battle, and won. What kind of assignments would he have to complete next? The thought of more adventure excited him, but for the moment, he was ready for rest. It was time to enjoy the time with his favorite human, Ralph. That indeed was his most important job, to sustain the boy's happiness and keep him safe.

Elt entered the doggie door, took a few licks of water, and walked over to and jumped on Ralph's bed once again. It had been an exhausting day . . . . and an even more exhausting week.

CHAPTER 17

Elt stared at the stars the next night, waiting for one to come closer and closer, that star being Coladeus's egg-shaped pod ship. Elt waited patiently, but he wondered if this was going to be the last time he would see Coladeus. Would there be another mission or was that it for him?

The day after all the excitement had been a quiet one. Sure, words around town were buzzing about the previous day's events, but in the Valleydale subdivision, all was calm. A few reporters from the Herald stopped by, attempting to get the latest scoop on how the animals rescued the town from Crum's men, but all of the neighbors, including Mr. Dawkins, who loved to boast about his Prince, were just happy to have their pets home. No one knew how the dogs disappeared. All they knew was that they were found at the Spring Valley National Bank, and had collectively thwarted a bank robbery. How the dogs got there and where they came from no human really knew. No human would have ever believed the truth of it all anyway.

Ralph still kept close tabs on Elt all day. He and his dog stayed close, either playing inside or outside together. He did meet Jenny just before dinner time for a walk. It was wonderful for them to go out for their walk and not worry about being in danger, although Jenny and Ralph were still a little cautious. They watched each car as it drove by, making sure their dogs were safe.

When Ralph was fast asleep that night, or so he thought he was fast asleep, Elt ventured outside to wait for Coladeus. A small, blinking light drew closer to Elt. It hovered a moment before landing in the same place it had landed last time.

There was a moment of silence, and then steam once again emerged from the ship. The door slowly opened and the familiar green light slowly illuminated the doorway. Coladeus slowly made his way down to meet Elt.

Elt bowed his head in respect for the Trianthian leader. Coladeus returned the gesture with a bow of his own to Elt.

Although the vessel landing generated very little noise, what noise it made may have been enough to wake a sleeping child. Ralph hadn't been sleeping soundly since Elt's disappearance. Even though his dog was home safe and sound, Ralph was still having trouble getting to sleep and sleeping soundly.

Whether it was a bad dream, a dry throat, or just a feeling that he was alone, Ralph awoke to discover Elt missing from the bed. Worried, yet still have-sleepy, Ralph wandered through the hallway and into the kitchen, deciding to investigate before waking up his dad. He could never have imagined what he saw next.

The kitchen was dark, but there was a strange greenish glow originating from the backyard. Ralph rubbed his eyes to make sure he wasn't seeing things. Ralph slowly drew the kitchen curtains open.

It was faint, for it was night, but it sure looked like his dog Elt was standing in front of a small egg-shaped ship, and there was a little green man talking to him. Wait a minute, that had to be a dream or something. Ralph moved over to the kitchen door and quietly opened it.

"So good to see you again Elt," said Coladeus as he reached out his hand to shake Elt's paw. "I wanted to congratulate you and your fellow members of your species for passing your first big test. You finished your assignment and passed with highest honors."

"But we didn't catch the main human who flew off in the flying bird machine," said Elt. "He left with one of the bad humans."

"Yes, I'm sure we will have to deal with Mr. Crum again someday," said Coladeus. "You and your friends did capture four of his men, including his strongest general. I am receiving reports from the next town over that there are many happy citizens who found out those men were caught and locked up in human cages. What's great now is that the humans from your town don't have to worry for now, and that means your species won't have to worry, but rest assured, there will always be someone new that could threaten your very existence and happiness."

The alien and canine were suddenly interrupted by a very confused and sleepy ten year-old boy.

"Elt, what are you doing boy?" asked Ralph.

Elt and Coladeus both turned around at the same time to find Ralph standing on the back porch in his pajamas. Ralph, Elt, and Coladeus all stood silent for a few seconds, but it felt like a few minutes. Ralph now realized that the scene before him was not a dream. He was too afraid to walk near them or turn around and run inside. Coladeus glanced back at Elt and shook his head.

"It is never fruitful when this kind of occurrence happens, but now we just have to deal with the situation as best as we can," stated Coladeus.

Coladeus then turned his attention to Ralph.

"There is no cause for alarm, no harm will come to you or Elt," said Coladeus, but the alien forgot to adjust his distransulator to the human dialect of English. All Ralph heard Coladeus say was a bunch of alien gibberish.

Ralph didn't understand what Coladeus was trying to relate to him, and retreated slowly towards the back door. Coladeus realized that he forgot to adjust his little machine, so once he set the dial to the correct language, words sounded much better.

"No need to be afraid," stated Coladeus. "I am Elt's friend, and your friend, too."

Still confused, Ralph stopped after hearing the alien communicate with him.

"Elt and I have been working together for quite some time now," mentioned Coladeus as he took two very small steps toward Ralph.

Ralph was still a considerable distance from the alien. Elt, attempting to both assist Coladeus and reassure Ralph that Coladeus was a friend, moved alongside the Trianthian in the direction of his human.

"I am Coladeus, from the planet Trianthius," said Coladeus. "You must be Elt's human. What is your name?"

Coladeus took another couple of steps toward Ralph, and Elt followed suit by doing the same. Ralph hesitated for a moment. He noticed that Elt was very comfortable with the alien. Elt had protected Ralph from bullies like Sam Meyers and bad guys like Frake and his men, so what was the deal? Was Elt under some trance or mind control? Ralph was still weary of the situation.

"Ralph," said the boy. "Ralph Eltison."

Coladeus slowly bent down and sat on the bottom step of the back porch. His glowing body illuminated everything around him, including Ralph and Elt. Elt followed and sat on the step between Ralph and Coladeus.

"I guess you wondering why I'm here in the middle of your Earth night speaking with Elt," stated Coladeus.

Ralph hesitated for a few seconds, still amazed at Elt's calmness around the alien.

"You can talk to him?" asked Ralph.

Coladeus smiled. "I haven't run into a language that I can't speak, with the help of this." Coladeus pointed to his distransulator. "Well, there was that time on that Spartan X planet," continued Coladeus. "I don't think those savages would have understood anyone."

Coladeus recognized Ralph's uneasiness.

"Please sit down Ralph," requested Coladeus. "In the short time I have, I will explain why I came here."

So, in just a few minutes, Coladeus revealed his planet's purpose in helping other civilizations, his role in all of the missions, and how and why he chose Elt to carry out the mission there in Spring Valley.

Coladeus explained Walter Crum's evil plot, and how all the neighborhood dogs were involved in stopping Crum. He told Ralph how Elt was captured, and how the other pets in the neighborhood rescued Elt and Bernadette.

Coladeus showed Ralph the small glowing stone on the inside of Elt's collar. He motioned for Elt to display a couple of the dog's new found talents. Elt obliged by jumping easily over the backyard fence into Mrs. Reed's yard, and then back over to his yard. Elt then sped around the house so fast Ralph couldn't keep up with him. Lastly, Elt lifted the log again and placed it back down with ease.

Ralph was amazed! This alien who he thought was abducting his dog was real, but the alien wasn't there to dominate the earthlings and their pets, but to help the human race.

"I must go for now, I don't want anyone else to discover my presence," said Coladeus.

"What about Mr. Crum," asked Ralph.

Coladeus rose from the steps and started walking back to his pod. Elt and Ralph rose also and followed the Trianthian.

"I'm sure we haven't heard the last from him," returned Coladeus. "His kind never give up. But rest assured, your town is safe now. Elt will grow wiser, stronger, and faster. He will protect your town and planet."

Coladeus climbed into the pod's doorway and stopped.

"There will be times here on Earth that Elt will be called upon to execute future missions, either somewhere on this planet, or very far away," stated Coladeus. "Like this past mission, it could be dangerous."

Ralph glanced down at Elt, and his dog returned the favor. Ralph placed his hand on Elt's head.

"Now that you know about Elt and his powers, you will be called upon to help him and maybe join a mission," added Coladeus. "But your most imperative job will be to keep Elt's powers and his contact with me a secret."

Ralph touched Elt's collar, pulled it back to reveal the stone, and placed his fingers around it for a second or two.

"I understand," said Ralph. "Yours and Elt's secret is safe with me."

"Good," said Coladeus as he reached out to shake Ralph's hand. Ralph shook the alien's hand. The Trianthian turned away and walked into his pod. The green glow disappeared as the door shut to the pod. Ralph and Elt backed away.

Emitting only a low hum, the vessel rose slowly into the air. Ralph and Elt watched as it slowly blended in with the star-filled sky.

Once the ship was out of sight, Ralph and Elt walked back inside the house. After a quick drink of water, Ralph returned to his room and collapsed onto his bed. Elt followed suit and crept into bed with his human.

What had just happened was too much to believe, but it was true. Was Ralph dreaming? An alien landed in the backyard and gave his dog special powers?

Ralph reached over and checked Elt's collar one more time. It was still there. Ralph bent down and hugged Elt. Even though he was excited, Ralph was exhausted, too. Before he knew it, Ralph fell fast asleep. It didn't take too much time for Elt to fall asleep.

The next day seemed like any other Saturday. The weekend in the summer usually meant yard work at the Eltison home. Ralph and Elt entered the kitchen together after a very restful sleep. Ralph fed Elt a stinky can of moist food. He didn't care, for his super dog deserved it. Ralph's dad cooked a giant breakfast consisting of eggs, bacon, pancakes, fruit, and toast.

"We're celebrating!" boasted Mr. Eltison as he served Ralph a whopping plate of food. "We're celebrating Elt's safe return, as well as the return of all the other pets. We're also elated that our town is safe again. The sheriff now has the four men and soon they'll be sent away and in a bigger jail out of Spring Valley."

Now Ralph's dad heard all the news about the dogs plus Jasmine catching Crum's men, but Ralph really wanted to set the record straight by telling him the whole story as he had found out the night before. Even his dad wouldn't believe him if he did tell, but Ralph had promised Coladeus not to tell anyone. So Ralph enjoyed the breakfast and kept silent.

While raking some leaves in the yard while his dad mowed, Ralph daydreamed. Yes, he hadn't daydreamed much since Elt had come into his life, but the events of the night before excited him.

Ralph could hardly believe it. His dog was like a superhero that could run fast, jump high, and lift really heavy objects. His dog could fight crime and send bad guys to jail. Coladeus said that he, Ralph Eltison, would be an important part of Elt's success. Maybe it meant he would be part of the team . . . . part of a mission.

"Ralph, you almost done with that raking, son?" asked Ralph's dad.

Ralph snapped out of his daydream.

"I'll be finished in a minute," Ralph responded.

Ralph continued to rake. He did finish his task, but couldn't stop thinking about his dog, the present he received for his birthday not even a year ago, was a superhero.

Ralph had so many questions for Coladeus, but the alien was gone and he didn't know when he'd see him again. What would Elt's next assignment be? Would he travel to far off places with Elt? It was overwhelming.

Ralph's excitement subsided a little after lunch. Jenny and Bernadette came over to play. Jenny too was excited, but just for the reason that her Bernadette was safe. Little did Jenny know that Bernadette had a special part in Elt's success, that although she didn't possess any special powers, she did participate in a couple of missions with Elt.

Ralph wanted to share the experience he had the night before with Jenny, but he knew he couldn't. Again, just like if Ralph told his father, Jenny would never believe him either. He knew that he had to keep his promise, but what seemed so simple last night seemed very hard that day.

Ralph decided though to give Jenny a taste of the secret without actually telling her.

"Hey Jenny, do you want to see what Elt can do now?" asked Ralph.

"Sure," Jenny replied as she sat down on the front porch steps.

"Watch this," said Ralph.

Ralph walked over to the fence in the front yard.

"Elt, come here boy," Ralph commanded calmly.

He touched the fence with his hand as he looked at his dog. Elt knew what Ralph wanted him to do. Elt ran, but in his normal speed. Almost effortlessly, but not making it seem too easy, Elt leaped over the fence, turned around, and jumped over it again back into the yard. He barely nipped the top of the fence with his tail. He could have jumped higher, or ran much faster, but he didn't.

Jenny smiled and clapped for Elt. Bernadette glared at Elt as he passed by her. She knew he wasn't supposed to show off his powers.

"How did he do that?" asked Jenny.

"Been training him," boasted Ralph.

"Elt really is a super dog," said Jenny.

"Thanks," returned Ralph. "Bernadette is pretty special, too."

Ralph had secretly shown Jenny a tidbit of Elt's powers without telling her the truth. Maybe one day Jenny would find out the truth about Elt, even about the missions that Bernadette was involved in. She only knew that somehow her dog and all the others wound up at the bank and helped stop the robbery.

The two kids played until almost dinner time, and then Jenny and Bernadette walked home. Ralph and his dad cooked out that night. Elt sat down in the grass and enjoyed the slight breeze that evening. The three stayed out until it was dark and gazed at the stars. Ralph and Elt both watched intensely for some sign of movement, wondering if Coladeus was traveling by. What mission were he and his crew on?

Ralph's dad went inside to clean some dishes. Ralph and Elt gazed a few more minutes before going in and getting ready for bed.

"Good night Coladeus, wherever you are," whispered Ralph as he walked up the back porch steps. Elt too was thinking of Coladeus as he followed his human.

As June ended and July began, Spring Valley prepared for another one of its big festivals; the Independence Day celebration. Once again the city park would be full of folks and their pets. There would be plenty of food, drinks, games, bands, clowns, and even a small parade downtown in the morning. At night the fireworks show would be the finale to a glorious day, with streams of red, white, blue, green, orange, and purple lights filling the sky.

The Independence Day celebration was also a joyous time for the town of Spring Valley. It had freed itself of the bad elements that had moved in and caused trouble. Folks were again safe and contented. Elt and his friends had helped the town, and the town was very proud of having these pets.

Although there was plenty of swimming, contests, games, and concerts, the major highlight of the day was the medals of Honor ceremony for the six dogs, one cat, and their owners. Mayor Helms decorated each pet with a shiny gold medal that hung on a fancy red band. Each pet proudly wore their medal on stage and sat proudly next to their owner.

Mr. Dawkins, Mr. Davis, Mrs. Perez, Mrs. Reed, Mrs. Yao, Jenny, and Ralph were also given certificates of honor.

"We owe a great deal of gratitude to these folks and their pets, for they accomplished an incredible feat by stopping four dangerous individuals," heralded Mayor Helms. "Without their efforts and bravery, we wouldn't be here today."

The pets and their owners gazed at each other. The owners, with the exception of Ralph, had no idea of the real story of what really occurred. First Bernadette was stolen, and then Elt was trapped. Jasmine's heroics of returning and organizing the rescue, the actual rescue, and the capture of Crum's men followed.

Was this the last time these dogs and cat would work together? Ralph had to keep quiet, keep his secret from his dad and Jenny.

As they walked down the steps, Ralph met his dad, who was gleaming with pride. Ralph's grandparents were at the ceremony and gave a hearty hug to their grandson.

Ralph had indeed come a long way. From a boy that was scared, lonely, and not very happy, to a young lad that found a great friend in Jenny. He wasn't afraid anymore, and even the lonely part disappeared. Sure, he missed his mom, he would always miss her. But in her absence, a very special element had filled the holes. It was his birthday present; a brownish-black mutt that no one wanted and was luckily found by Mr. Drexel.

Elt was a super dog, even without his powers. Ralph knew it. Ralph knew that there was more to his pet. He enjoyed his dog every day. He loved the walks, the fetch games, and nights on the living room floor playing with his dog's tug-of-war sock or favorite red ball.

The days that followed would bring new adventures for Ralph and his dog, whether it was helping their town, their planet, a civilization far away, or just a pretend game with his best friend ever in the back yard . . . .

ABOUT THE AUTHOR

Dan grew up in Newport News, Virginia and attended Virginia Polytechnic Institute and State University. He has devoted nearly thirty years to the motion picture exhibition industry.

Dan has enjoyed writing all of his life. He has written numerous screenplays, one which was pitched to a major movie studio in 2003.

When Dan was ten, he wrote a story dedicated to his childhood dog "Trixie." Years later that story inspired him to create "The Adventures of Elt the Super Dog."

Dan now resides in Frederick, Maryland. He is married and has three sons.